For Michael whose praise means the world to me. I hope you enjoy this.

Susan

The Speed of Light

by

Susan Pashman

THE PERMANENT PRESS
SAG HARBOR, NY 11963

Library of Congress Cataloging-in-Publication Data

Pashman, Susan.
      Speed of Light/by Susan Pashman
          p.   cm.
      ISBN 1-877946-86-9
      I. Title.
      PS3566.A77285S64   1997
      813'.54--dc20   96-3048
                                   CIP

First edition, August 1997

THE PERMANENT PRESS
Noyac Road
Sag Harbor, NY 11963

To Mark R. Nathanson
for his widsom, his compassion and for the inestimable
gift of Time.

ACKNOWLEDGEMENTS

This book emerged in the Ashwagh Hall Writers' Group with the sure, knowing midwifery of Marijane Meaker. Her astute professional judgment and sturdy personal encouragement guided the writing, which was fun, and the long march toward publication, which certainly was not.

My colleagues in the group provided the patient listening and thoughtful feedback that can save a writer from solipsistic madness. The group itself, by its warmth and good fellowship, furnishes what is truly a spiritual home for its members.

Particular thanks to Stacey Donovan, vanguard and validator; to Vince Lardo for his unerring sense of narrative structure; to John Andrews for his imaginative musings on astronomy; and to Diana Peate Semlear who taught me about dancing.

Carolyn Krupp at International Management Group, by her unflailing enthusiasm and faith, urged me through the final, most difficult, stretch, and my editor, Judy Shepard, somehow guessed at all that had gone into this book and treated it with the intelligence and tender respect every writer hopes for.

Odd, to discover that what seemed for so long to be an utterly solitary process ends with gratitude to so many. Odd, but quite pleasurable.

And remember that the companionship of Time is but of short duration. It flies more quickly than the shades of evening. We are like a child that grasps in his hand a sunbeam. He opens his hand soon again but, to his amazement, finds it empty and the brightness gone.

Meditation, by Y. Pennini from the *Siddur for the High Holy Days,* Isaac Gluckstein, trans.

PART ONE

One.

He had fallen asleep reading, in a familiar posture. Head back, mouth agape, one of those sculpted fish standing on its tail, its mouth a fountain. Gravity weighed on his uvula and pulled his tongue backward, closing his throat, and he stopped breathing. But in a moment, his head fell forward and his jaw slammed shut. The bite of air restored him and his head lolled back again. And so it went.

Behind him, French doors opened to the terrace overlooking Gramercy Park and the first silky strands of coolness to wend their way through the stolid remains of a swampy September day. There was still enough moisture below to throw gelatinous halos around the streetlamps. Nineteenth-century streetlamps, full of charm, that his wife's committee had installed around the park.

A night of soft-edged lights. A dampness that turned the white squares of windows on tall buildings to the south into swimmy splotches. A dampness that made the illuminated baroquery on the bank building a huge damaged wedding cake, its icing smeared about, its finely stenciled details indistinct. Narrow ribbons of coolness wove past the chipping paint on the French doors and teased the back of his neck. He gulped at it. His head lolled onto his shoulder. The book in his lap shut itself and slipped between his knees onto the living room carpet.

Carla was a round-assed fetal lump beneath the covers. Sturdy Slavic calves, large suntanned knees pulled up to her bosom, and all of it wrapped in white cotton printed with baby pink roses. A handsome Tartar face, wide-boned and bronzed, burrowed deep into the pillow. A limp old pillow that needed rearranging several times throughout the night. His pillow lay lifeless beside her. She slept carefully, even in his absence honoring the unspoken covenant never to allow so much as a toe across the imaginary line down the middle of their bed. But even in her careful sleep she was grateful for the flat empty space beside her and for the silence of it. Her shoulder pressed into the lumpy mattress, savoring his absence from their bed. The absence of his gasps, his glottal rumblings, his lurchings.

The baby pink roses on her thin wrapping sweetened her sleep. She believed in the power of delicate barriers. She knew that simple faith fortified them, making even a cotton nightgown into armor. She swam among the roses as she fell to her sleep, unreachable, impregnable. Even if he had wanted to touch her, he could not. Such was the efficacy of her faith in delicate barriers.

He could no more touch his wife than he could swallow a bolus of squills. Those mornings when he woke beside her in the dark, he sometimes considered the mountain of buttock and imagined slipping a hand between her thighs. The shiny umber curls on her pillow, the taut sunburnt cheek still appealed to him. But his hand died on its way to her, bested by the rose-printed nightgown.

He could not even wish she slept nude. The plump mound of ass he had once, briefly, adored had lost its shine and its scent. She was a density bereft of definitive line, an irksome contemptibility. Until dawn, when he hurried to close his eyes and make his mind blank for awhile before arising, he recounted endlessly the reasons his hand could not traverse the distance to his wife's thighs.

If he woke beside her and found his bedlamp still lit, he could study her as she slept. Her face, her face! It might almost make up for the rest. It was still a rosy, sweet freshly-plucked apple, ripe as afternoon sun. Full lips, full lids, opaque blue eyes beneath a dark, serene brow. A large round bowl brimming with fruit. Peaches. Plums. Blackberries. Her face held the memory of the first time he had seen it.

The coral impatiens on the terrace straightened on their stems. The air through the French doors was cooler now, dryer. He stopped breathing again, gagged, and resumed a raspy snore. In his dream, something small and hard had hit him in the chest. Larger than a bullet, smaller than a fist. A tennis ball moving relentlessly into his chest. His chest was very thick. The ball could not pass through. His chest was molten rubber. The tennis ball lodged there. He should not have played tennis that day. Not on Yom Kippur.

He wondered if God had witnessed his insolence as, after services, he shed his navy blazer and tie and slipped into his tennis whites. Every gesture, he knew, had been too abrupt, too furtive. And now there was a tennis ball in his chest, a thick menacing knot. "You fool, Dr. Kline," the voice of God was saying, "nothing escapes my eye."

He lifted his heavy lids, leaned forward in the chair, and stared at the book on the carpet. Magazines scattered on the floor. Stacks of magazines Carla still could not throw away. Despite her recent resolve. Boxes of magazines lining the dining room beyond. Things she simply would not throw away. The tennis ball could not pass through his chest. He closed his eyes and made it a dream again. A tennis ball pressing inside him.

Nathan knew his game was in irreversible decline. Even Carla could beat him at singles now. A woman. A woman twelve years his junior, but a woman. Open-heart surgery two years ago could not restore his game. The feeling in his hands and right arm returned but his stamina never did. Carla was a damn good player. Always damn good. Not so terrible these days to lose a match to Carla. Worse to lose to Tom, that no-class entrepreneur. Tom, who bought designer graphite racquets before he could play tennis and a silver lamé ski suit before he learned to ski. It was enough losing Carla to Tom. Losing to Tom on the courts was unbearable.

He shouldn't have played tennis today. Not on Yom Kippur. Not in that heat. Fasting and playing tennis. But he beat him, that bastard. He beat Tom at singles. And now the tennis ball couldn't get through. Tom had a killer serve. The man who had made love to Carla for so many years, the man Carla said she really loved, had served a tennis ball right into him.

He rose and walked onto the terrace. It was a touch of angina. It would pass. The clock on the bank to the south said five past eleven. Years ago—how long was it now?—

15

Carla had asked him to look at a sore. An ugly sore. Tom, good old Tom, Nathan thought, was a great guy. A guy with a warm, happy handshake. Street-smart, direct. Nathan had envied the fearlessness that could let a man be so direct. And modest. Almost apologetic for the serendipity that had made him unspeakably rich. Tom gave Carla herpes. He never told her he had it; he just gave it to her.

Carla loved him anyway and that was what she told Nathan even as she begged him tearfully to examine the oozing sore. She told Nathan she loved Tom anyway even as Nathan was running his finger around that dark wet cave of hers, positioning the bedlamp the better to see the runny pustule. He didn't care just then that his wife loved Tom. He was nauseated by the sore. He set the bedlamp down on the bed and walked silently to the bathroom to scrub his finger. There were faint ripples like chills in his jaw.

He was sure it was Tom's serve that had landed the tennis ball in his chest.

It was just angina. Maybe a bit strong because he'd worked so hard to return that serve on a hot, sticky day. It would pass.

The air conditioner in their bedroom had a chronic moan. Carla had her chin tucked down. The blue blanket pulled up over her face was pilling from too many washings and the satin hem was shredded. She still hated replacing things, still hated spending money, never threw things away. Her shiny brown hair floated above the shredding satin blanket hem. The sleep of the safe.

She was safe with Nathan. He kept a safe distance. Their fights were fought obliquely. She had married him to be safe. Her father, her mother too, had pressed her to do the safe thing and when it was done, she let the safety engulf her as a November fog. She slept, chin tucked down, a safe, foggy sleep. Nathan remarked to himself for the thousandth time upon the soundlessness, the motionlessness, the perfection of his wife's sleep. He imagined she would sleep the same way if she knew what was happening to his heart.

It would pass. He went back to his book.

The letters grew large and then small on the page. He wanted to throw up. He returned to the terrace and studied the white splotches on the buildings south of Gramercy Park. Carla, he concluded, would be fine. She still had that face. She would marry again in no time. Probably another doctor. Doctor father, doctor husband. Second doctor husband. Doctor husband the second.

Nathan wondered who it would be. The face that was a bowl of fresh ripe fruit. The elegant carriage, the European breeding. She would be safe again in a year or two. A man would sigh and long for that face. A man who had not had her would be lured by those huge, unresponsive breasts as he had been. A man might imagine he could arouse her even now, even thirty-four years later.

You know a good tennis player after one or two strokes. And a skier, moments into a run. You know a thoroughbred at a glance. A moment's conversation. A conversation overheard. Carla would be fine.

It was twenty past midnight on the clock south of the terrace. The tennis ball had become his whole chest. His chest, his arm, were wound tight into one huge pounding ball. Hard and pounding as Tom's killer serve. It would be embarrassing showing up at the emergency room, a doctor, so far advanced into a massive coronary. They would ask why he'd waited so long.

He would wake his wife. She would drive.

Two.

You know a thoroughbred at a glance. A moment's conversation. A conversation overheard.

The elevator door closed before he realized that this building he was in had no twelfth floor. And so, in 1955, Nathan Kline, recently returned from the navy, rode to the ninth floor, entranced by a radiant fresh-apple countenance, dark curls, and a waist made tinier by the full bosom and hips that bloomed around it. She was abundance, he thought, glossy, fragrant, vital. She saw only the elevator operator and addressed only him. All Nathan's senses yielded to her. She filled the elevator car, she overflowed it and filled the shaft, the building, the wrong building!

Nathan had meant to be in the building next door but now he was lost in a sound, a perfume, a presence that stunned him into alertness even as it clogged his consciousness. By the time the elevator reached the ninth floor, the reverberations of her tutored English, the mannered modulation of her voice and the undeniable lilt of it were the noontime bells in a tiny town of churches, all pealing at once and making him delirious.

Her composure, her self-assured gaiety. She was loved, indulged. She spoke of her holiday from college. She would be returning to Smith on Sunday. She nodded pertly to the elevator operator and looked straight ahead as she left the tiny car.

As they descended to the lobby, Nathan managed to pay the elevator operator five dollars for her name. Carla. A name as round as an embrace, round as a bowl. A bowl brimming with peaches, a bosom bursting with nectar. Not English, but tutored in England, Nathan concluded. A thoroughbred. Weisenthal. German or Middle European. An old-world thoroughbred.

Next day, he rode the subway to Columbia and flashed his alumni card at the guard in Low Library. The Smith College Yearbook. Weisenthal, Carla Wei-sen-thal. Junior Class Secretary. Daughter of Dr. Felix and Sophie Weisenthal. Born, Prague, 1937. No siblings. Brearley. Art History major. His cheeks burned. His head bent closer to the page as he strode past the bookshelves with the automatic movement of a panther on the scent.

Her father was a doctor. They would talk about medicine; they would talk about Europe. They would be colleagues. Nathan imagined Felix Weisenthal a lean, slight man not unlike himself, a man of great wit and the sort of encyclopedic learning one expects of educated Europeans. He would appreciate Nathan's refinement and erudition in a way Nathan's own father could not.

Nathan saw Felix Weisenthal delivering his luscious daughter to Nathan and watching with amused approval as Nathan ravished her expertly: Nathan plowed and strove as Dr. Weisenthal cheered him on, admiring his skill and endurance and emitting a small giggle when his daughter finally moaned. Nathan held his briefcase in front of him to hide what he supposed was a hugely apparent erection and hastened to the men's room.

He returned to the Broadway local, shuttled crosstown to Grand Central, and walked to the hospital. His office was dim, spartan, but in the right part of the basement. He was immensely pleased to have an office so near to the research labs. He had had superb training here in New York and then in Switzerland at the war's end. The navy had let him stay on under Kopfer, caring for refugees. Ophthalmological surgical techniques yet unheard of in New York. He had credentials, contacts, he could let anti-Semitic remarks pass. They had assigned him an office in the research area. His star was on the rise.

The dark blue spine on the *Directory of Physicians and Surgeons* was new, stiff. It crackled in his palm. Felix Weisenthal. Born: Prague, 1899. Certificate in Psychiatry, Vienna, 1928. He would have known Freud. Freud would have known him. Nathan was already deeply connected to him by a powerful lust for his daughter. Nathan's lust for Felix Weisenthal's daughter was no mere yearning, but a tidal swell that washed over the three of them, binding them irrevocably. It defined a project, an undertaking so immense in its reach and significance that Nathan would have been thoroughly overwhelmed had he not been so certain of its outcome.

Some thirty publications in German. Prestigious journals. Nathan was pleased that he could recognize the names of the finest German-language medical journals. Two books in English. A thoroughbred. He had known it instantly. But, of course, that's what a thoroughbred is.

He snapped the *Directory* shut and stood slightly bent, hips thrust forward, running his right hand through the fine reddish blond hair he'd inherited from his father. It was a habit he wished he could break. The gesture brought his father too close, reminded him that his flesh, his bones came from that man.

Bone, Nathan thought, is what his father was. Dry, dusty bone. Not a moist drop of joy in him, he bent grimly to his daily labor, never pausing to enjoy its fruits. A successful enough accountant for all it mattered. Nathan's brother, Irv, was an accountant too. Two dour, mirthless, fiercely competitive men. And Nathan, the frivolous younger son, or so they said. Indulged by his soft-hearted mother, they said. She spoiled him, made him a sissy. Not just Irv and his father, everyone in the family said that. But his mother stood up for him, defended his taste for European culture, his love of fine music, his fondness for tennis and skiing. Irv lifted weights which, the senior Mr. Kline was quick to point out, was an efficient, cost-effective way to stay fit. Whenever he ran his hand through his fine red hair, Nathan worried that there was more of his father in him than he realized, worried that he might not have escaped after all.

He was staring at the floor now, envisioning a plum, a plum dangling from the very top of a tree. He was, in his own way, as competitive as Irv and now he was on fire. He was, at that moment, Nathan of unstinting determination who had bested all the gentiles at Columbia's School of Physicians and Surgeons. He was Nathan Kline whose skis could carve perfect edges into the sheer ice on Tuckerman's Ravine.

He set the blue *Directory* on his desk and drew a sheet of bond from the top drawer. He sat down deliberately as a man who must come to terms with some stunning, momentous news. He fumbled in the top right drawer for the fountain pen he had received from Dr. Heaney upon completing his internship. He leaned forward as he did when surveying a particularly difficult ski slope, grasped his pen firmly and fixed his gaze upon the whiteness on his desk, readying himself for the torturesome twists of Tuckerman's Ravine.

"Dear Miss Weisenthal," he wrote.

"I confess it is with some embarrassment that I address this note to you. A young lady of your obvious fine breeding might certainly be shocked to learn that I obtained your name from the elevator operator at 40 East Sixty-second Street shortly after having had the splendid good fortune to travel all-too-briefly in that elevator with you last Saturday. No doubt you have forgotten me if, in fact, you ever noticed. . . ."

He crumpled the paper, lit a cigarette and began again.

"Dear Carla,

"Who can say what draws a man to a woman? A man of considerable experience, I have had the good fortune to have traveled extensively in Europe while in the navy. I hope you can forgive my immodesty when I congratulate myself on my excellent intuition for, you see, I glimpsed you only briefly in an elevator the other day and yet I knew immediately that. . . ."

And again:

"Dear Felix. . . ."

For godsake! Perhaps he'd been at it too long. He rose and walked around his desk, letting his eyes come to rest on the blue *Directory*. Perhaps it was a better approach after all. She was his only daughter, his only child. Hadn't he fled Europe with her in his arms? He would want an appropriate husband for her. Someone learned and impressive. And Nathan did, he had to confess, have a yearning for Felix. As much as he wanted Carla Weisenthal, he longed to be embraced by her father.

Or, on the other hand, he might write to her mother. A mother might be won by an older, protective man, someone cultivated, well-placed. Women had, after all, always cozened to him. He settled himself in his chair again. "Dear Mrs. Weisenthal," he began. "Chance is sometimes the kindest of friends. . . ."

He returned to "Dear Miss Weisenthal" and stuck with it through a pack and a half of cigarettes and several excursions to the men's room and the faculty cafeteria.

"Dear Miss Weisenthal,

"I write in the hope that you will, in time, forgive this brazen stroke. Although I admired you from afar at a party we both recently attended, I failed to request an introduction. Now, I have only regrets, for the indelible memory of you exhorts me to make your acquaintance at last.

"I am a not unhandsome man of 31, an ophthalmological surgeon and a member of the faculty of New York University's School of Medicine. Having completed my training at the University, I was fortunate to have had the opportunity of additional training under Dr. Karl Kopfer in a navy medical center in Geneva for two years prior to completing my tour of duty.

"Who can say what draws a man to a woman? I know only that I departed from a casual visit to an old friend in Massachusetts regretful at not having insisted upon an introduction to the most attractive girl in the room.

"I am not, I assure you, accustomed to being so importunate. However, I know no other way to compensate my regrets but to write a brief note requesting an opportunity to introduce myself to you personally.

"I hope you will not reject this unusual request out of hand but, rather, consider it and discuss it with your friends and, of course, with your family. If you should see your way clear to allowing us to meet, you may write to me at the address on the enclosed card. I would be most grateful for your telephone number so that I might call to arrange the necessary details.

"Wishing to assure you of my absolutely sound intentions in this regard, I have attached a list of professional references which you or your father should feel free to check at your leisure.

"I look forward to hearing from you and, again, beg you to forgive this unseemly approach to the matter.

"Sincerely."

Nathan attached his professional resume and three references and reread the letter several times before sending it off.

That evening he visited Sylvia Rubinoff, a lusty Communist nine years his senior, whom he'd met at a lecture at Cooper Union. There were large chipped bowls brimming with thick lentil soup and irregular grainy slabs of bread and a greyish brown crust around Nathan's mouth when he was done with his meal. Sylvia's throaty laugh amid the pillows and feather beds pricked his inventiveness. Her big pink belly thrust at him from every direction. He was a tiny splinter of a man, caught in her golden thighs until morning.

Three.

Radiant, glossy Carla Weisenthal was not in love the way her classmates might have been. Hers was a quiet, abiding love for a man at Yale who played superb tennis, sailed a splendid boat, and never touched her. She dated others, of course, and sometimes let them plunge their tongues into her mouth when they said good night. It was unpleasant, but she had learned at Smith to gargle with mouthwash immediately upon returning from such evenings and so it was an unpleasantness quickly forgotten.

Always smooth-shaven and crisp in tennis whites or sailing whites, Philip Neuman was the man Carla would have beside her, within her, all about her for her lifetime. But it was not the whiteness of him. It was, in fact, his darkness. It was the blackness of his eyes, the rumbling ambiguities in his demeanor, the unanswered questions. It was the interstices that she filled with her own hopes for him that made him so irrevocably hers. He was irrevocably hers because she had invented so much of him.

She had written his name in various styles of handwriting along the margins of the notes she took in General Biology, and had sometimes written "Mrs. Philip Neuman," which she thought would look excellent in print. In her Sophomore year she'd written, "Dr. and Mrs. Felix Weisenthal take pleasure in announcing . . ." But when, after a tennis game, she ran, flushed and glowing, to the net to meet him, he stopped a few paces away, taking her into his eyes and smiling a soft, sad smile.

He met her at New Haven station when she arrived for homecoming and drove the Studebaker to Haven House. He carried both her bags to a third floor room all pink and white with marguerites and daisies on the walls. He had brought her to that room before. As before, she sat in the rose damask armchair, its rusted springs creaking, while he unpacked her clothes, respectfully hanging each skirt and blazer in the ample closet, cradling her cashmeres to the dresser as if setting a sleeping infant in its bassinet. And then, as before, he propped the pillow against the headboard and swung his long flannel-trousered legs onto the bed.

He spoke of his roomate. "Mike will be taking Natalie to the game, of course. He could do without it, but Natalie wants to be part of everything. You know how she is. How most girls are. I'm very, very lucky to have you."

Carla's eyes moved momentarily from her lap to his face and caught the sad smile. "The game is just an excuse, you know. Just an excuse to be here. To see you again."

They passed the afternoon in the places they had initially assumed: he, elongated upon the bed, she, in the oversized chair, her hands folded in her lap, her blue eyes sometimes darting hopefully to meet his and then modestly retreating to her lap. He asked about her paper on Brueghel. She asked about his Comparative Anatomy exam. And was that fellow still sabotaging other students' slides in Microbiology? And then, sailing. It was growing cold. He'd be going up to Groton next Saturday to dry dock the boat. And his mother, was her hip healing? The gentle laughter they shared about their mothers who had both come from Europe and could never really be American, even if they had bobbed their hair. And what would she be wearing tonight?

"The powder blue wool suit. Is that okay?"

"You know I love that suit. That color was made for you."

Nathan's letter waited for more than two weeks on the starched linen runner on her bureau at 40 East Sixty Second Street, sandwiched between an invitation to the Brearley Alums' Christmas party and a newsletter from Henry Street Settlement. As it was a real letter, she saved it for last. By the time she finished reading it, she had stepped back from the bureau and sat down numbly at the edge of her bed, bracing herself against the slippery surface of the taffeta bedspread. She wished she had never let it out of its envelope.

"Mother! Mother?" She found Sophie Weisenthal in the dining room. "Mother." Carla extended her arm with the letter just barely held between her thumb and forefinger.

The letter that had alarmed her daughter utterly charmed Sophie Weisenthal. And the letters of reference! The resume! She smiled up at Carla.

"You remember him from the party?"

"I don't know what party he means! I don't know who he is! I don't know how he knows me! What should I do, Mother?"

"I think we show this to your Papa. The man is a doctor. Maybe well-known. At dinner. Papa will decide."

Felix Weisenthal's soup grew cold in the wide-rimmed bowl while he studied the papers in his lap. For months he had lain awake nights forming the sentences he would need to help his daughter see the truth without causing her pain.

"Carla, my darling," he would have to begin. "This

25

Philip from Yale is a very lovely fellow. But you must understand that as a psychoanalyst I can see things that remain hidden from others. It is because I love you more than my own life that I have to tell you to leave this man alone. He cannot become a husband or a father. He is no man for you, my lovely daughter, because he is no man for anyone."

Felix was dismayed at the prospect of invoking his professional wisdom to sway his daughter's affections. He tormented himself with this dilemma for months. And now, this letter, this Nathan. This Nathan was an exceptional man.

He took a few spoonfuls of the tepid consommé, lifted the papers from his lap to the table, and continued pensively until the bowl was drained. With his linen napkin, he dabbed the droplets of soup from his bristly mustache and rested his round, balding head in both his hands.

"This is an exceptional man," he said finally. "I will check the *Directory*, but I think you must write to him tomorrow."

"Papa! Are you saying I should meet him?"

"Of course you *must* meet him. We must *all* meet him. This is a very exceptional man. The kind of man you must meet."

Carla excused herself and ran to her room. Sophie looked steadily at her husband. Early in their courtship, she had seen a German rendition of "Felix the Cat" and had ever since called him "*Katte*."

"*Katte*, I think perhaps you rush to judgment. No one knows this man. Where he comes from. What kind of man he is. This may be dangerous."

"I said I would consult the *Directory*. If it would give you more comfort, I will also ask around. I have a feeling people will know this young man. They will have heard of him. I'm sure I am right about this."

"Your daughter could never say no to you," Sophie told him. "You suggest something and it's an order to her. Now you are going too far. You frightened her this time."

Felix rubbed his forefinger back and forth across his

mustache. "The man from Yale is no man at all and she is too much in love with him," he said. He turned back to the letter beside his plate. "This Nathan is exceptional."

They waited in silence while the maid served their dinner.

"Importunate," Felix resumed. "He uses such language. 'Importunate' is a wonderful word. Only a highly cultivated man would use such a word."

When Nathan called her, he said things he had rehearsed very carefully and she agreed to an afternoon at the Metropolitan Museum and invited him to lunch first to meet her parents. Nathan's anticipation drove him wild. He almost bowed when Sophie introduced him to her husband.

"You know," Felix Weisenthal beamed, "you and I are probably the only two men alive who actually use the word 'importunate.'"

Four.

There is a shade of lavender reserved for November dusk. Blue enough to herald December when there would be no dusk. Rosy enough to console the brown leaves that still cling to their branches. A lavender sky, streaked shamelessly with orange, stretched out at the western edge of Central Park.

Her eyes were watery with cold and her cheeks crimson with it. She pressed forward against the evening chill, her hands buried in a fur muff that suited her so perfectly Nathan could have leapt to embrace her when he saw her with it. But he kept his reserve.

"You look more charming than ever," he said with a narrow smile. Nathan enjoyed this measured pursuit.

"Thank you. I guess winter's just about here."

Impersonal conversation. She was demure, perhaps coy. She was playing her part of the game, he supposed.

She supposed she was seeing him for her father's sake.

27

This exceptional man, this Nathan. There were times she took pleasure in his company, times when his quick wit could make her laugh. Other times, she would try to imagine him in some cozy place, in the guest house in New Haven, perhaps. In silent conversation, words exchanged in glances. When she tried to imagine him in these ways, she found it was Philip Neuman she was imagining, not Nathan. Nathan always spoke at great length and she had to admit she rarely heard it all. Phil spoke very little, but she remembered every word and repeated entire conversations to herself after they'd parted. Repeated them as she curled about her pillow, nuzzling the soft linen. Repeated them to the oval mirror framed in rock maple that hung over her bureau in Barnes House. She pressed herself against the cool plaster wall, her cheek, her hips, her open palms, and the tender underside of her arms.

At Christmas, Nathan bought her a silk scarf from France the color of her eyes. He took her to the Brandenburg Concerti and offered a critique of the trumpet solo that seemed, to her, quite brilliant. He took her to tea at the Plaza and to the Impressionists at the Modern. She blinked attentively through his disquisition on Manet's uses of the color red. They drove to Peekskill for a weekend with her parents.

The Weisenthals' country house sprawled on a soggy plateau in a slope from the road to the lake, a huge slumbering mutt: mangy, arthritic, loyal. Former owners had tugged it this way and that, adding wings, enclosing porches to create long, drafty, many-windowed rooms and then slinging new porches around the perimeters of the old. It had no discernible shape inside or out.

Felix had torn out the little hive of servants' rooms in the rear wing and made for himself a barny retreat, stocked with sagging couches, insufficient lamps, and low tables where open books lay nesting in others. There were no shades or curtains on the broad, new window that overlooked the lake. A maze of passages and stairs led back to the original house with its tiny upstairs bedrooms and poorly plumbed baths.

Nathan sat amid chintz cushions in the meandering living room. Embers hissed at his back from a massive stone hearth. He and Felix drank vodka and talked late into the night about Medicine, about Prague, about Vienna. He sat with Felix at the window that gave out across the snowdecked lake and drank coffee and talked about St. Augustine, Blake, and Pascal. He asked Felix about the psychology of visual perception, about Gestalt theories of perception, about Kohler and Koffka and Arnheim. And when Felix asked him about optics, he was ecstatic. A colleague, Nathan thought. A worthy friend at last!

On Sunday afternoon, Felix played a recording of Bach's A-major violin concerto.

"Ah, Bach. My favorite," said Nathan. "And the A-major violin concerto with its brilliant coda. How nice of you to play it."

"Wolfgang Schniederhan," Felix said with his ear cocked to the record player.

"Excuse me?"

"The violinist. A Viennese not so well known in the States, but one of my favorites," Felix said.

"Ah," said Nathan. "And who is conducting?"

"I believe it's von Karajan." Felix raised his bushy eyebrows and peered over his glasses at the record jacket. "Yes, it is," he said, checking the record jacket. "With the Salzburg Festival Orchestra. What do you think of Schniederhan?"

"Excellent, excellent," Nathan replied. "And here is the second movement. A theme that returns in the coda."

Felix shut his eyes and leaned even closer to the record player. "Ah yes, you are right," he said after some consideration.

Nathan surveyed the field of snow spread out upon the lake. His remark about the coda had more than made up for his ignorance of Schniederhan, he was sure. In the end, Felix had been dazzled. This richly learned man was worth

29

impressing. A challenge with a bountiful reward, Nathan thought: his chatty, pleasant wife, his glowing daughter, a superbly cultivated family. Nathan held fast to the moment to still the pangs of anticipation.

The piney forests ascending the mountains around Northampton were spongy underfoot. Reservoirs of melted snow seeped from beneath the brown pine needles and gushed over hiking shoes that zigzagged happily up the mountainside. From a mossy platform of mica-flecked rock, Phil Neuman extended an arm to Carla, anchoring himself with his other arm wrapped around a limber birch. She was breathless and beautiful when he drew her up beside him on the slippery moss. Flushed and laughing and panting. She was wondrous. He bit the forefinger of his damp suede glove and withdrew his hand. It was her eyes he wanted to touch. He wanted them to be hard as the two aquamarines they appeared to be. Hard enough to press in his hand, to press to his mouth. He stroked her cheek and kissed her lightly at the temple.

Here, Carla thought. Here on this smooth glacial rock, this rock of ages embedding a millenium of worms and beetles! Let it be here in this meager March sunlight while only the pines are green, while our noses are running and raw! Here, with our hiking boots on!

Phil slipped his hand into hers. From their perch atop the mountain, the tiny clusters of clapboard buildings and ivy-covered red brick were bits of painted marzipan. The Holyoke Range rose umber and grey before them. They strained and squinted to find the pond at the rim of the Smith arboretum.

"Just one year left," Carla said.

"I wish _I_ still had one year left," he said. He would start medical school at Tufts next fall. Carla was anxious. Tufts was nearer Northampton. He might visit more often. She was certain he would not.

Nathan visited Northampton, but he did not care to

climb the mountains. On his first visit, Carla brought him to Chez Luce, a cheery, raftered place reminiscent of a chalet. Luce relied almost entirely on white wine and garlic for seasoning, but the ambience appealed to Nathan and he was happy to return to Chez Luce each time he visited.

"We could go somewhere else if you'd prefer," he would say. "Of course, I do love their frogs' legs. And the sweetbreads, too. But if there's someplace you'd prefer . . ." Carla would say it didn't matter to her, which was true.

"You really do love exotic food," she remarked one evening after they'd told the waiter their order. "You'd like those chocolate-covered ants my friend Cora's mother always sends."

"I do like to indulge my palate," he said. It saddened him when he thought of it and he stared wistfully at the tablecloth.

"My father," he continued without looking up, "is very abstemious. A staunch Puritan, that man. Eat to live, don't live to eat. What a drab life he has." His lips pressed hard against his teeth. Finally, he sighed and smiled up at her. "I'm the prodigal younger son, you see. I'm not expected to amount to much."

They both laughed at that and he knew he'd finally touched her.

In the autumn of Carla's senior year at Smith, Phil's letters were long and frequent but his visits were neither. Nathan was permitted to fill the emptiness. He would tell her how his practice was growing, how complicated hospital politics were, how good it was to see her.

Nathan had thoroughly won the hearts of Felix and Sophie Weisenthal by then. Scores of accomplished Europeans had swept through the house in Peekskill that summer and they were full of congratulations. Sophie and her sisters embraced Nathan and the men guests winked at him. A promising young doctor, well-placed, well-spoken, and so well educated for an American! They had heard his father was a certified public accountant with a solid clien-

31

tele in New Jersey. And the brother was a lawyer _and_ a certified public accountant! Felix was a fortunate man. Sophie was a fortunate woman.

Nathan began arriving at Northampton each week after Friday tea to take her to dinner. One late October evening, he drove with her to a spot near the arboretum. He brushed her curls with his fingers and gazed down at her. Oh, gorgeous, radiant Carla, when can I ask you? he thought.

Carla resisted the dry rim of his lips when he leaned forward to kiss her. She sat still, breathing evenly, and let his hands rest on her bosom while she breathed.

"Could we do without the gloves this time?" Nathan asked gently. She had extracted from her purse a spotless pair of white cotton gloves that he knew would smell of Clorox when they got wet. She'd explained that all the girls at Smith wore gloves for hand jobs. _He'd_ explained that all over New York, Europe, everywhere, girls grabbed hold of men's cocks with their bare hands, and sometimes with their mouths. She had looked so young, so frightened, staring down at her lap, he hadn't had the heart to press her.

But this time he said, "Carla, let's try it just this once. Some girls get to like it very much, you know. Even Smith girls. Your friends are surely doing things they don't tell you about."

Her knees were pressed tightly together, her gloved hands resting upon them limply. He stamped wet, terse kisses on her neck, trying to distract her as he unbuttoned the periwinkle cashmere cardigan. He released the clasp at her back, eased her brassiere up to the strand of pearls about her throat and leaned back to gaze upon it all. Gourds, he thought. Immense decorative gourds. The kind with demarcations so sharp they appear unnatural. A sharp divide where a summer's tan ended, another sharp divide at the borders of the large, rosy nipples. More than he could bear. He thrust both hands out to cup them but there was so much more than they could hold. He placed his hands about one of them and buried his face in it.

"Oh, Carla, please!"

She closed her eyes, slipped off her glove, and did it with her bare hand. She left the wet hand in his lap, unable to take it back in that condition.

"Ah, you are so good. Thank you." Nathan tenderly kissed her neck, then her brow. "Ah yes, your hand." His left hand groped in his pocket and found nothing. He took her hand in both of his and wiped it on his shirt. He hoped his laughter would make her laugh too, or smile. And there was a tiny smile that never parted her lips but a smile nonetheless and it heartened him.

Five.

The Harvest Ball. It would be Nathan this year, not Phil. And a grey-blue peau de soie gown. Philip loved her in that shade of blue. But Philip had ebbed away just as Felix had said he would. And so it would be Nathan this year.

Nathan looked forward to meeting her friends. Ronnie Lebenthal, a roommate who had had her nose fixed. Cora, whose mother sent chocolate-covered ants and who had just had an abortion. Grace Nussbaum, who had embarassed herself attempting to seduce her senior-thesis advisor.

Nathan would wear the tuxedo he had bought in Dusseldorf, he told her. Mohair. So close a weave, it felt like steel. Never creased. It would outlive him.

A week before the Ball, he took her to the dinner-dance for the Pediatric Wing at the Medical Center in New York.

"Well, here I am!" he'd trumpeted, bursting into the Weisenthals' library. "And here," he cried, parting the flaps of his topcoat as though they were curtains opening on a puppet show, "is the Dusseldorf tuxedo!"

Sophie helped him off with his coat and Felix circled about, admiring the suit. He stroked the stiff lapels. "You won't get another one of these," he laughed. "Wear it in good health! Carla, my darling, come see what your remarkable boyfriend is wearing tonight."

"Very handsome," she said, and handed Nathan her wrap.

At home, later, in the Weisenthals' kitchen, Carla made some coffee.

"Nathan, I hope you won't wear that tuxedo next weekend. You do understand, don't you?"

"Actually, I'm afraid I don't."

"Oh, c'mon Nathan. You're being obtuse. Please, just wear a regular American tuxedo."

"Why?"

"Why? Because you look like the Kaiser in that outfit, Nathan."

"Oh really, Carla. Just because it's German . . ."

"You look like a German. A stuffy old German. Please, Nathan. Please don't wear it when you meet my friends."

Nathan said he would take it under consideration.

He arrived at Northampton early the next Friday. Luce offered a dry Chablis with the frogs' legs and Carla spoke enthusiastically of a poetry reading at Amherst. Tomorrow night. Intriguing people. Robert Frost and a reception to follow at the English Department. She had managed an invitation from Ronnie Lebenthal's brother, a junior member of the Department. It would be a very special evening. Far better than the Harvest Ball. And no need to lace up in all those stiff clothes.

And then it was Christmas again. Arpeggios of crystal wine glasses and brandy snifters. The virtuoso harpsichord trill of the Telemann Trio Sonata. Tintinnabulating sopranos against a continuo of altos as well-wishers greeted each other in the Russian Tea Room. The Hallelujah Chorus. A thick frenzy of bodies racing up and down Fifth Avenue. The resplendent cascade of counterthemes as Bach's *Pasacaglia* reached its crescendos. Parties, friends. Nathan's colleagues from Columbia and from the hospital. Carla's school friends. Hors d'oeuvres, champagne.

Stew Abrams, Nathan's roommate at Columbia, became engaged to an Englishwoman he had met in Europe during the war. Maxene Paulsen-Quine. Nathan admired her. Virtually everyone from their class was at the engagement party. Nathan passed the evening with the physicists who, in undergraduate days, had formed a little clique on the top floor of Livingston Hall. Their enthusiasms had engendered Nathan's devotion to Baroque music.

"The physicists are the true geniuses of our class," Nathan used to tell Stew.

Marvin Lampert was a physics major who commuted to Columbia from the Bronx because he could not afford to live in the dorms. It was Marvin who had unravelled the mysteries of the Bach A-major violin concerto for Nathan, demonstrating how the theme of the second movement wove back into the coda. Baroque music, Marvin had told him, is what physics would be if it were music. Complex. Intricate but orderly.

Lew and Marian Perrin were at the party too. Lew had studied literature at Columbia and gone directly into his father's jewelry business. It was a pity, Nathan told Carla, because Lew was really a poet, a rare bird with one foot on the Earth and one in paradise. Lew had chosen to live on the Earth. But after they'd had dinner at the Rainbow Room with Lew and Marian, Carla remarked that she couldn't discern a jot of poetry in Lew. She liked him for being so down-to-earth, and she liked the effervescent Marian even more.

Dr. and Mrs. James Heaney invited Nathan to their Christmas party. "Gorgeous," Heaney whispered to Nathan when he was introduced to Carla. "Delightful girl," Mrs. Heaney said and offered a claret for the partridge blanketed in buttery pastry.

Cora's abortion had resulted from an encounter with a Princeton man, Henry Sedgwick, whose mother hostessed a Christmastime bridal shower for Cora at the Princeton Club one afternoon. Nathan picked Carla up at five. She introduced him to Cora and to Ronnie Lebenthal and Grace Nussbaum.

"Thank you for arranging the invitation to the Robert Frost event," Nathan said to Ronnie. "A really enjoyable evening."

As they drove away from the Club, Nathan said that Cora seemed too nice for Henry Sedgwick and that Ronnie's surgeon had taken off too much of her nose and that he was surprised Grace's thesis adviser hadn't had the sense to take her up on it.

"Really, Nathan!"

"Yes, really. She's not you, of course. Nothing of your aristocratic charm. But she's very attactive nonetheless." Grace Nussbaum, Nathan thought, was attractive in a troubled and a troubling sort of way. The sort of way a man does not forget.

On the last afternoon of 1956, they stood in a queue outside the Criterion Theatre under one of those light wet snows that become transparent a foot or so above the pavement. Carla had wished for a frothy Hollywood movie: *Around the World in Eighty Days.*

"Carla?" A baritone voice was taking her into its confidence. She caught just a glimpse of the lithe form behind them and made hasty introductions.

"Philip is in medical school at Tufts," she told Nathan. Nathan asked a few questions about the faculty, enough so the younger man could grasp his seniority.

"Phil played first singles for Yale," Carla said.

"What sort of racquet do you use?" Nathan inquired and manuevered the conversation back to a comfortable place.

"You were awful to him," she told Nathan as they were leaving the theater. "I used to go out with him, you know."

Of course, Nathan knew.

"How did you know that?"

"Your color changed," he said. "Anyway, I'm glad you threw him over for me."

"It wasn't quite like that," she said.

"Whatever you had to do to make room for me," Nathan

said, "I'm glad you did it. I'm very happy, Carla. I think I might turn out to be one of those rare creatures: a truly happy man."

She did not answer him, and Nathan took this as sufficient assent. He put his arm around her shoulder. "Yes," he said, "I think it just might turn out that way."

That evening, Sophie sat at the foot of her daughter's bed, stitching down a fastener that had come loose on the black velvet bodice of Carla's best gown.

"The same thing happens with my evening gowns," she told her daughter. "We ladies with the big bosoms, we always have these problems. The men don't understand this. They just go crazy for the big bosoms."

Carla stroked the dark red taffeta skirt. She knew she had run out of time. The cacophony of winks and nods, knowing smiles, and pinched cheeks was reaching its climax.

"I really can't marry him, Mother. I can't."

"I was very nervous like you when I married your father," Sophie said, giving her daughter's knee a sympathetic squeeze.

"I'm not nervous," Carla protested. "It's not that. Mother, he's really too old for me."

"Twelve years is a good distance between a man and a woman. He has advanced nicely in his career. He will take good care of you, you will see."

"It's not the twelve years, Mother. It's just the way he is. He's too old for me."

"Papa almost loves this man." Sophie looked embarrassed.

"I know. I know Papa loves him. He's an old-world European just like Papa." Carla reached across and stroked her mother's cheek. "I love Papa," she said, "and I love you too. But I don't love Nathan, Mother. I can't."

Sophie bit off the end of the thread and laid the gown across the foot of the bed. "You will love Nathan someday too. You will see. It takes time, the love that comes in marriage. Take a nap, *liebchen*. It will be a late night for you tonight. But wonderful. Papa and I will wait up. I, myself, should take a nap."

Carla stared at the voluptuous rolls of deep red taffeta. The thick black velvet of the bodice. She fingered the little fastener her mother had lovingly sewn in place and she sat back on her bed, drawing the cool pillow against her chest. Papa was a very good, a very wise, man. And he loved her, wanted the very best for her. She could never doubt that.

She pressed her fingers into the deep velvet and ran them down to the slippery taffeta. She realized for the first time the power of delicate barriers. She realized that simple faith could fortify them, making even a bit of taffeta a mighty suit of armor. It would make her unreachable, impregnable.

He would ask her tonight and, unreachable, impregnable, she would say yes. And, yes, unreachable, impregnable, she would marry him. She would wrap herself in a comforting fog. She would marry him in her sleep.

Six.

In cream-colored linen Bermuda shorts, purchased expressly for the occasion, he paced impatiently before the hotel window. It was true, he thought, the sand *was* coral. A color more obscene than beautiful as it reached the blue of the ocean beyond. The raucous clang of their impact had so impressed the hotel's decorator that the two colors were forced to collide over and over throughout the Honeymoon Suite.

His brand-new wife was bolted in the bathroom.

"Carla, darling, it's been forty minutes. Are you ill?"

"I'm all right. I'll be out in a few minutes. Why don't you find the bar and have some Rum Swizzles? I'll be right down."

When he returned an hour later, he found her coiled in a

clump of pillows, tears spilling over the apple cheeks onto a blue-and-coral flowered spread. The room was rank with the odor of ripe cheese.

"I'm sorry, Nathan. Something awful's gotten to my stomach."

After four days of it they flew home. To Peekskill. Sophie put her daughter to bed. Felix thought it might be distress about the marital act.

"Oh, I'm sure it's not that," Nathan said.

Six months earlier, Carla had been fitted with a diaphragm. There had been times in the car, in motels, and in the sprawly house in Peekskill, when he'd kissed and fondled her enormous breasts, searching for the spot, the gesture, the tempo that would arouse her. When he'd been so wild with desire just gazing at her that he'd had to hum a Bach cantata to himself, stroking, caressing, and kneading until she acquiesced. She was sick with fear, this beautiful young wife of his, but it was not so small, so precise, a fear as Felix imagined. She was young, Nathan told himself.

He carried the crates up the narrow stairs, despite their incommodious sizes and their considerable heft, as though he were lifting a ballerina, supporting them past three stories on just the tips of his fingers. He opened the door of their tiny top-floor apartment with a push of his toe and moved with some urgency to set them down upon the table. He'd had to make several trips but his precious Rosenthal china, service for twelve, was home at last. Exercising every privilege at his disposal, he had still had to pay dearly for it in Germany and pull all sorts of strings to have it shipped to America. And after all that, he'd almost had to forfeit it.

"How does a husband come to choose the china?" Carla had demanded to know one afternoon in Peekskill. Nathan had just described the comeliness of the Rosenthal set. His allusions to Attic restraint, "The Horse of Silene," for example, had set Sophie in a swoon.

"It's my wedding gift to you," Nathan had said.

"But you didn't even know me when you bought it!"

"That's true. I bought the most elegant dinnerware imaginable," he'd said, "and set about finding a woman worthy of it."

"I wouldn't have chosen plain white."

"Rosenthal is the very finest," Sophie had agreed. And here it was. Ninety-six pieces, plus servers.

"Are you going to have a look?" Nathan asked.

Carla helped uncrate a few pieces and ran her hand across the cool creamy glaze.

"They really are very elegant Nathan. Thank you."

She stacked the crates on the floor of his closet and, when she had filled that space, stacked the remaining crates beside his dresser. It would remain Nathan's china.

He studied his wife of three weeks. She moved about their apartment in the same cardigans and pleated skirts she had worn in college, folding yesterday's newspapers, covering bedsheets with a spread, lining kitchen drawers with flowered paper. Her gestures were indecipherable, obscure. He studied his wife as she went about setting napkins on the table and for the first time he wondered what she was thinking. Suddenly, then, he understood that he would never know that. In her unfathomable otherness she could elude him utterly. She could keep herself in purdah; she could deceive him. It struck him that he had possessed her more perfectly before their marriage, before it ever occurred to him to wonder what she was thinking.

Her face was lustrous as ever, the aquamarine eyes shone as fiercely. But she moved in an hermetic, sequestering fog, a thick November fog. She was in his room, in his bed, and yet she was in fog. He slid his hand beneath the rose-printed flannel nightgown, over her hip and into the warm place where one of her breasts rested upon the other. But she arose in the morning and carried her breasts to the kitchen where they were a bewildering, fluctuating swell beneath a navy wool robe, something he remembered in another kitchen with the bland aroma of cream of wheat. He was disturbed by the transformation of her breasts. He disliked the kitchen and kept away. The fog confused him. Her varying forms confused him. The kitchen confused him.

A book party for an author she had edited. She had volunteered their apartment with its rooftop garden. "Much too formal," she said when Nathan suggested the Rosenthal china. Important people would be there. A brilliant young man from Newark who'd had a story in *The New Yorker*. She labored over canapés and spread crackers with colored creams, smoked oysters, and red and black caviars; they huddled self-consciously on silver-plated trays.

Nathan tended bar, passing lavish compliments and delectable quips as generously as he poured vodka. A senior editor invited him to play tennis. The brilliant young writer would bring his father for an eye examination. An author whose name he could not remember would send him an autographed copy of something.

His cousin Lily arrived late with her husband, Howard. Two psychiatrists, they each saw patients late into the evening. Lily had been his first, when he was fourteen and she twelve. It was not a fact he recalled about her as he would have recalled something she said. It was the very gist of Lily, her name; it was indigenous to the merest thought of her. Howard was distracted and disarrayed as ever but he managed to congratulate Nathan once again for winning Carla. Lily requested a teaspoon.

Nathan searched the kitchen cabinets and drawers. He felt bumbling, oafish. He pulled out a drawer lined with flowered paper. Knives, forks, tablespoons, three large serving spoons. They apparently had no teaspoons. He proffered a tablespoon which Lily accepted gratefully.

"Carla, darling, where do you keep the teaspoons?" he asked when the guests were gone and they were toting bags of refuse to the incinerator.

"In the drawer near the stove."

"Which drawer, sweetheart? Left or right?"

"Left."

41

He opened the drawer. A plastic tray with four compartments. Butter knives, salad forks, teaspoons, canapé forks. "Carla, why aren't the teaspoons and the tablespoons in the same drawer?"

"I keep the big things in one drawer and the little things in the other. It's easy to remember that way."

Nathan knew he would never search for silverware again. He would improvise somehow if he were ever alone in the kitchen. He considered that he would live the rest of his life with a woman who kept teaspoons and tablespoons in separate drawers. Would he have married her had he known that about her? He wondered, too, if he'd have married her knowing that for several hours every third day or so she would be bolted behind the bathroom door. The chase was concluded, the quarry secure, and Nathan was left with the irreducible otherness of his wife. At that moment he was utterly alone. And terrified.

Within a few months, heaps of papers lined their bedroom. She saved every issue of the *New York Times*, five weekly magazines, medical journals that he had finished reading. The crates of Rosenthal china.became buried under piles of *The New Yorker*. On her lamp table were the manuscripts she read each evening, plowing through them for something promising. Suddenly, it seemed, she could not decide what to say about them. She read aloud to him. His responses were judiciously ambiguous. She grew furious with him: He was erudite and impressive, but she would not be able to defend or even to explain his remarks. He was no help at all! She reconstituted herself and began scribbling and jotting. Her confidence in her own judgment was diminished. She was yielding more of herself to him than she realized.

He had proposed a ski trip to celebrate their first anniversary. She had demurred. She had never skied. They could try Bermuda again, she had suggested. Now, he leaned backward, his elbows jutting out crazily as he made his way up the narrow staircase, a mountain of bags and boxes artfully counterpoised against various parts of his body. He sashayed deftly to the table and and let them tumble from his arms.

"Presents, sweetheart. Anniversary presents, if you will." All in all, Nathan was pleased with himself.

The familiar glossy red paper and the gold insignia of B. Altman. Bags and boxes. Her eyes roved the tabletop, seeking out the smallest parcel. A slim bag. Lingerie, perhaps. She unfolded the contents. Long, white flannel something. Long underwear. A larger bag. Three cotton pullovers, grey and brown and cerulean blue. The largest box with its loops of gold ribbon. A hooded jacket, brown and pale blue.

"Bogner," he beamed at her. "The best in Europe. In the world. Try the leggings, sweetheart. It's all coordinated. You're going to be a terrific skier so you have to look terrific. Oh Carla! You're going to look gorgeous in this! You really are a thoroughbred. I knew it at a glance."

Carla resigned herself. "I'll try it," she told him. Then she tucked the leggings and pullovers into her dresser and hung the jacket away. She folded the red paper and the gold elastic cord into the boxes and stacked them on top of the pile of *New Yorker*s.

They had been married one year. He had, he told himself, tried very hard. To know her, to anticipate her needs, to please her. But the Rosenthal china, the handsome ski costume, his fingers gingerly probing her clitoris—they were all, he decided, a lot like the teaspoons in the kitchen: Everything seemed to end up in the wrong place.

Nathan wondered if other marriages were like his. He considered their pretty apartment with its rooftop garden, the friends they were beginning to share, the dinner parties and cocktail parties they had arranged, the vacation they would take. To others, he concluded, this surely must seem a perfectly happy marriage. He decided that things were, most likely, just as they were supposed to be.

Seven.

Alexandra Devorah Kline (born November 16, 1963, weight: 7 lbs. 2 oz., height: 19 inches), was conceived in Kitzbuhl on a ski holiday. Carla had become a passably good skier. Plucky, but never dancerly, Nathan said. He would accompany her, instructing, coaxing, encouraging, along two or three runs and then deposit her at the hearth where she chatted while he tested himself against the harshest slopes. It had been Carla's fervent hope that motherhood would bestow a final dispensation from skiing.

"Oh, *Katte*! She looks exactly like Nathan!" Sophie cried, pressing her face to the nursery window. And there was no mistaking it: The ruddy, mottled knot of wrinkles would eventually resolve into a not-very-pretty little strawberry blonde.

"God should have let her favor her mother," Felix murmured to his wife.

Nathan watched as the nervous little jaw chomped erratically on his wife's nipples. He watched as Sophie cradled her granddaughter in her arms and sang fragments of a German lullabye. He felt proud, and then guilty in his pride. He'd had, he knew, almost nothing to do with it. This noisy, squirming bit of protoplasm that had entered his home, warming it like some rich infusion, came from a woman. And its glow belonged, he decided, mostly to the women. When he considered it further, Nathan finally concluded that the birth of his daughter, instead of revitalizing him, had moved him along in the chain of being and thereby taken some of his life *from* him. He felt measurably older, denser. He was the older generation, now. Responsible, grave. Once more, he worried that he might turn out like his own father. He vowed to himself that he would not.

Still, the sun had crossed its apogee. Nathan wanted to reach up his arms and push it back to that place in the sky just before noon, to the spot it had occupied before Alexandra arrived. He wanted to stretch out his fingers and keep the sun from starting its inevitable descent.

"It's a miracle," Felix said, his eyes riveted to the tiny pink face. "There is no other way to account for it. A miracle is what that is." It was not what Nathan would have expected from his father-in-law.

"Actually," Nathan chided the older man, "there's a perfectly scientific explanation for it and if you'll leave the women and come to the kitchen for a drink, I'll explain exactly how she got here."

Felix followed Nathan to the kitchen. "Maybe I'll have a cup of coffee," Felix said.

Nathan had never attempted to use the percolator, to assemble its half-dozen parts; it required too much time in the kitchen. "For coffee," he said, "you'll have to wait for Carla. Why don't we have some vodka?" He set two glasses on the table.

"It *is* a miracle, you know," Felix resumed.

"Well, it's very nice," Nathan offered.

"No," Felix insisted. "It's important to have miracles. Very important to see mysteries for what they are and to say to yourself, 'There is another mystery, another miracle. Right here in my own life!' That's how I kept going in Europe before we got to England."

"Really, Felix, I never imagined you were religious. Do you still feel that way?"

"Not religious, Nathan. Humbled."

"But you are a man of science."

"But that is precisely it, Nathan. The miracle is what is given, it's the premise from which we 'men of science' proceed. First there is consciousness. Then, we begin. You with your physics and chemistry, I with my analysis."

"You amaze me, Felix. Have another vodka. What is it you are calling a miracle?"

"All of it! All of it! I am perhaps too emotional. Still, you have to agree that consciousness, anyway, is inexplicable. Alexandra's funny little face that looks like you, you can explain that scientifically. And her bony head and what will be, I am sure, a prodigious brain. There will be satisfying mechanical explanations for those things. But of con-

45

sciousness and its contents, we will never know more than
we do right now."

"You have so little faith in science, Felix. Why so pes-
simistic?"

"But it is the very opposite, Nathan. It is the sublimest
optimism. That consciousness is beyond the reach of scientific explanation is surely cause for celebration!" He
drained the vodka from his glass. "A cause for optimism, at
the very least."

"Felix, you amaze me and, I must confess, you disappoint me a little too," Nathan said. "We're not very far
along in the history of predictive science. Time will yield
far more in the way of explanation than we have now.
Science is getting there, Felix."

"But it will never reveal the origins of consciousness or
its contents." His plump hand reached for the vodka and he
dribbled a few more drops into his glass. "Your probes and
lasers may someday count the molecules in Alexandra's
brain, and measure their electrical properties, but you will
never know her thoughts except by the account she gives.
The brain's chemistry, yes. But consciousness itself will
never be the subject matter for chemists." He drew the clear
liquid into his mouth, held it a few moments, and continued.
"Dreams and languages, illusions and allusions, yearnings
and terrors, these are beyond the reach of chemistry,
Nathan. They will always remain miraculous. The existence
of life itself is miraculous. In fact, the existence of anything,
rather than nothing. . ."

"Now, Felix, this really is going too far."

"Think about it," the older man said. "You will laugh
out loud. Miracles will make you very happy, Nathan.
That's my secret."

"I'll give it a try," Nathan said quietly. He studied his
empty glass. He ran a finger around its rim. He was bewil-
dered by what he had discovered in Felix.

"And now, I would like to have some coffee, Nathan.
Get my beautiful daughter, would you? And thank you,
Nathan. Thank you for my miraculous grandchild."

As the dark fragrance of coffee settled over them, Nathan regarded his father-in-law happily chatting in the kitchen and he knew he would never believe in miracles, much less be cheered by the thought of such things. A searing grief pierced him as he reflected on this. Pain that was part envy, part isolation. He would have to forgo the embrace he'd so hoped for from Felix.

A cold, bright November morning. The sunlight in precise parallelograms on the carpet of his consultation room. He was more than halfway through his allotted three score and ten, on the cusp of forty. He had a thriving Park Avenue practice, a baby daughter, and friends and acquaintances whose names meant something. He had a famous father-in-law and an enviable wife. His father had been wrong: He *could* indulge in the pleasures of a refined and cultivated life and be successful in his work as well.

Doris Needham, a widow, kept his files meticulously, ushered patients smoothly through three examining rooms, sent out bills, kept the books, remembered Carla's birthday and their wedding anniversary and the birthdays and anniversaries of all his relatives. She suggested, and even bought, appropriate gifts. Nathan moved from one examining room to the next, reading the cards she set out, making pleasant banter, endearing himself to those afflicted with glaucoma or cataracts. He listened intently to their complaints and replied with heartening quotes from Virgil or Marcus Aurelius. They adored him. He paused every hour or so for a sip of tomato juice or of Stolichnaya. It was not at all a bad life he had.

But as the days passed and he returned each evening to his wife and their baby daughter, the sense grew within him that he was not living as fully as he could, that he was not doing all he was capable of doing. His practice was humming now without his putting forth much effort. The excitement of Alexandra's arrival had subsided and whatever it was the women of the family did with her now did not include him. He could not allow himself to die this way, he thought.

He should climb through the ranks at the hospital. Chief of Ophthalmology. He doubted they would let a Jew become chief. Columbia College had let him be valedictorian. But then, he'd made it impossible for them not to. There were, he knew, more subtle considerations in getting to chief. Certainly, he was charming, affable. Too charming and affable, perhaps. Patients came to him for second opinions and stayed. Patients he saw at clinical rounds showed up at his office. His practice expanded at the expense of his senior colleagues. At the expense of Heaney himself. And Heaney had let him know he was aware of it. Over claret and pheasant in buttery pastry. The way gentiles let you know things. There was a shriek. And commotion in the waiting room.

Doris Needham kept her starchy dignity as she knocked on his door. "The President's dead," she said. "He was shot in the head. In Dallas. Mrs. Horowitz just came in and told us. The patients are very upset. Would you like to speak to them?"

"We are all sorrowed by this news," Nathan said, addressing the distraught little group in his waiting room. "If you would prefer to reschedule your appointments, Mrs. Needham will accommodate you."

Lily's office was beige. The walls, the carpet, the velvet upholstery, the lamps. There was a soft, whirring sound in the waiting room and that, too, was beige. On that particular evening, when Lily buzzed him in, she sat deep in a huge beige chair, her platinum pageboy all Lana Turner, backlit by a very fashionable lamp, and Lily was beige that evening too. Her lipstick was all chewed off. She had been crying. He took her to dinner and back to the office and they undressed and vanished into the beige.

"It's a shock, you know," she said afterward. "I may be too traumatized to see my patients tomorrow."

"It's been a terrible day," he said. "I sent all my patients home. Mrs. Needham rescheduled everyone. She really is so efficient."

"He was so young. She's so young. That makes it so much more tragic. And the children! My God!"

"Past forty is not young. It's pretty far along. I'm past forty and I've never been president of anything."

Lily lit a cigarette and stared at the ceiling. She was depleted.

"I was thinking of talking to you when the news came. What do you think of my moving up at the hospital?"

"Moving up?" Lily was drifting.

"To chief."

"How?"

"There are several ways. What do you think?"

"You're Jewish, so you'd have to be Einstein. You'd have to find a cure for cancer. Or have a project that brought millions in research money to the department. Why do you want this? You have a Park Avenue practice, a new family. For godsake, Nathan! You have an enviable life, and it's just beginning."

"It's not enough."

"Is it boring?"

"It's too small."

"Too small?"

"Too small to be my whole life."

In the elevator down from Lily's office, he thought of Carla. It seemed he had not thought of her for quite some time. He leafed back through his day. Chief of Ophthalmology. Heaney. The assassination. Lily. He had come to Lily to talk about his plan. He had been unfaithful to his wife, but it hadn't seemed that way. It was Lily, after all, not some new adventure. Lily had been there since . . .well, since childhood, for chrissake. It was not, he concluded, an act of adultery. It was Lily.

He was not suited to hospital diplomacy, that was true enough. He would find a research project. Millions in grant money coming into the hospital and him as head of the project!

Lily was a genius. It certainly wasn't adultery.

49

Eight.

The kitchen windowpanes fogged with aromatic steam. Steam bearing scents of garlic and onions and a roast's juices spattered about the oven. The tawny fragrance of pecan pie, the blossomy perfume of *apfelkuchen*, and, sunk down in the bass notes, the peasant-footed smells of turnips braising and potatoes roasting. The floors of the old Peekskill kitchen sloped toward the center of the house so a shelled pea dropped on the floor rolled nearly to the dining room. The room itself, so often rearranged by its various owners, had an indeterminate number of corners. Corners that folded protectively about the women bent to their work.

Sophie and Felix lived in the house year-round now, and Nathan and Carla came up on weekends with Alexandra. Sophie's longtime housekeeper was Hadassah Kimmel. "Hassah," Carla had called her as a child and the name had stuck. Hassah kept a timeless Maine coon cat named Gustav. The women chatted through the kitchen steam— Sophie, Carla, Hassah, and Alexandra, who squatted on the low end of the floor, feeding Gustav the peas that occasionally rolled off Sophie's lap.

"He wants to be department chief, Mother."

"I told you he would be very successful," Sophie said.

"He's a brilliant man," Hassah said. "And so nice with this little girl of his. Surprising in a man like that, don't you think?" She prodded Carla's arm. "We wished the best for you and you got it. The best husband!"

"Thank you," Carla said. It had been foolish to try to discuss Nathan's ambitions with them, her fears that the small thing that remained as their marriage might vanish entirely.

Felix rushed in brandishing a sheaf of crayola drawings. The artist had labored prodigiously over her signature, sending it around corners where necessary to fit in all the letters. A-l-e-x-a-n-d-r-a. There were large, fat circles in torpid repose atop massive rectangles. Some circles had whiskers. Some rectangles had tails.

"You see how she has distilled the very essence of Gustav," Felix exclaimed. "Picasso worked a lifetime to achieve such purity of form." He brushed the peas away from Sophie to make space for the drawings. "What is Gustav? He is smug. And smugness is a fat, round circle, of course. And what is his hulking presence but a monolithic rectangle! The quintessential Gustav! I love a child's vision. So pure. So absolutely right!" He danced into the dining room, stooping to sweep Alexandra up in his arms. "Picasso? Bah!" he said, planting a kiss on her nose.

The guests arrived. New friends, old friends. Shaking off the January snow. Harrumphing to expel the cold, inhaling to savor the warm. Embracing their hosts, shedding parkas and handing up bottles of wine. They all arrived at once, twenty minutes past the stated hour, so that the narrow vestibule forced a stream of them into the living room, some still clutching hats or gloves.

"Ah, this big old hearth is a pleasure." Robin Colby shoved a fistful of almonds into his large, wet mouth and thrust his hands toward the fire. He was a huge, coarse-featured man with a moist pate and gnarled limbs.

Nathan proffered a drink and cautious conversation about their shared profession. Robin was the group's *enfant terrible*. Aberrant, dangerous.

"This house is always a pleasure in winter. Look at the moonlight on that icy lake." Melancholic Armand Ackerman was Carla's favorite. Despite the polished smile that flashed across his chiseled features, Armand's quiet manners hid deep and ancient wounds. He would always be inconsolably lonely. Some said the only explanation of his marriage at forty to the frowzy, alcoholic Zoe Langton was her Mayflower heritage, but Carla would not permit gossip about it.

Zoe poured herself a double Scotch and sidled along the piano to where Tom and Tilly Szabo were waiting for their drinks. The Szabos had just arrived in Peekskill; the dinner was in their honor. Zoe had heard that Tilly was the daughter of a Tennessee horse breeder. She hoped this new woman, a gentile in her second marriage to a wealthy Jew, might offer rescue from the isolation that was Zoe's lot in the group. But Tilly's project, it turned out, was to succeed with Tom where his first, Brooklyn-bred, wife had failed. Tilly was struggling against her nature to learn to cook and keep house and have more tow-headed babies than anyone could count. Zoe poured more Scotch and continued along the piano to find the Perrins rapt in Felix's discourse on the significance of a child's artistic representations.

"The intuitive vision that cuts right to the essence of a thing, that distills perception down to its pure meaning, that intuition is utterly miraculous. Miraculous because an adult like Picasso has to work for such clarity but in a child, well, it just appears!" The old man beamed at Marian Perrin. "You are a happy woman, I can tell," he said. "Your husband loves you and that puts roses in your cheeks."

Marian smiled at him benignly.

"I know what I am saying," Felix insisted with a chuckle. "I, too, have the intuition of a child."

"Dinner, everyone. Take any seat. Boy, girl. Szabos in the center so we can all get to know them." Carla was a scrupulous hostess.

Everyone knew the purchase price of the Szabos' new home. What they wondered was what Tom did to afford it. They were grateful for Marian Perrin's radiant good nature. It allowed her to ask directly.

The compact, barrel-chested Hungarian was the son of a Brooklyn tailor. "It was public school all the way," Tom said, gesturing expansively. "No ivy crawling over *me*." He had sniffed the company enough to know what distinguished him from almost everyone at the table. And he knew his frank admission would startle them and win him further distinction.

"I guess you're wondering how a kid from Brooklyn College ended up with the Hale Estate. Well, I certainly didn't inherit it." Tom's eyes, like his smile, were full of mischief.

Carla felt uneasy with her guest of honor. His sincerity challenged her other guests, shifting the compass that usually steered their dinner conversation. It left her unsteady, off balance.

"I won a sixty-million-dollar law suit," Tom said. His absurd grin and raised eyebrows told them that, like them, he was astonished by his fate. Now he was one of them.

Szabo had spent some army leave in Hungary on a quest for his roots. He'd struck a deal there for a patent on a synthetic fiber that could be woven into virtually impermeable textiles. He licensed the patent to the government for spacesuit construction, they exceeded their license, and Tom sued. Some of the sixty million went into a development company.

"What are you developing now?" Nathan was curious.

"Oh, holography, cancer cures. You'd be amazed at the nutjobs that knock at our door. I'm never going to find that fiber again, but I have to keep trying. Have to keep running. Brooklyn guilt, I suppose."

Tom sensed he'd had enough of the spotlight. "What's your game?" he turned to Lew Perrin.

"Jewelry," Lew said, "and I *did* inherit it."

"We're expanding into Tibetan art," Marian added.

"Marian bought a wooden sculpture in Tibet last winter that was too ugly to have in the house. I used it in a window display at the store. You wouldn't believe how many people wanted to buy the damn thing."

"So we sold it," Marian said, "and then everyone wanted one. We're going back next month for more."

"Hey, you never know," Tom said. "When I bought that fiber, I was thinking swimsuits."

"Robin, please! Not while we're eating!" Reena Colby's protests were in vain. At the far end of the table, her husband was well into his story.

"Well, the Germans were minor news in France at first," he was saying. "There were such juicy scandals to divert attention." He reached for his wine with one thick hand and for another slab of beef with the other. "The roast is splendid Carla, and," he paused for a noisy swallow of wine, "I love braised turnips. Americans underrate turnips. So these two were found dead in the office of the Minister of Culture," he continued. "The aristocrat, slumped over his desk with blood running from his mouth onto the desk blotter. The other, crumpled on the floor in a pool of blood which seemed to spring from his upper thigh."

"Rob, please!" But Reena had to capitulate. All ears were bent to Robin.

"The aristocrat had a hematoma high over his left ear and there was a heavy glass paperweight on the floor near the other fellow's hand. The aristocrat had died of a cerebral hemmorhage. They often drain into the mouth, you know. The police hypothesized a fight in which one took it in the leg with a letter opener or something and retaliated by smashing the other's head with the paperweight. I could have told you that was ridiculous given the quantity of blood."

"Robin, I think your wife is right," Armand said. He wanted only to register his distaste. There was no hope of diverting Colby.

"When the medical examiner went looking for the wound to the fellow on the floor, it turned out he was bleeding profusely from the crotch. And . . . his penis was gone! They looked in his pants, on the floor. Nothing. Then, they examined the fellow with the hematoma and what do you suppose they found in his mouth? Voila!

"Apparently, the aristocrat had been sucking this poor slob off and had gotten too rough, so his partner whacked him on the head and inadvertently killed him. As his chin hit the desk, his jaw clenched shut and he chomped off his lover's penis." Robin thumped his massive fist on the table and laughed until he began to cough.

"For Heaven's sake, Rob!" Reena Colby held her napkin up to her face.

"The government tried the usual cover-up but the papers got the story. The French were so enthralled with the scandal, they ignored Hitler for months."

Reena helped Carla clear the dishes. "I'm sorry about Robin," she said.

The guests said good-night. Nathan slumped among the chintz cushions. "Colby really makes me sick to my stomach," he began. "And, you know, he'll always be part of the group. Goddamn son of a thief. Father runs to Switzerland and changes his name from Goldberg to escape the goddamn Feds. Robin returns to the States with a waspy name, a Swiss education, and a degree from the Sorbonne and marries Rustin Klieger's daughter. He gets Klieger's practice, the best ophthalmology practice in New York, and all the Klieger money. And here's what kills me: That crass bastard is in line to be chief at Saint Luke's! They think he's a goddamn French-educated wasp!"

Nathan stood up and slammed a chintz pillow into the sofa. "He's a pig," he continued. "He fucks Chinese girls, and you know what? I think he fucks Chinese boys, too. And now he's going to be goddamn chief!"

Carla had heard most of this before. The news about Colby's nomination as chief registered only as a troublesome lump, an unpleasantness she would become accustomed to. Nathan would curse and complain about it for years, she supposed.

When she was a girl, her father had taken her to see the bears at the Central Park Zoo. It was the only time she'd actually seen a bear, but she knew there was a bear dancing in the kitchen now. A barrel-chested Hungarian bear, twinkly-eyed and roguish. She inhaled deeply as she sorted through the silverware. At the very least, there was a bear-fragrance filling the Peekskill air that night, wafting in, she decided, from the delicatessen streets of Brooklyn. She felt alert, expectant, some new rhythm had been set in motion.

Nine.

On Alex's fourth birthday, Nathan bought her a harpsichord. He had always longed to play the *Well-Tempered Clavier* on a proper instrument. Stout, woolly-haired, and solemn, Alexandra doted upon her father and he upon her. Although he could not explain it, Nathan was delighted that the little girl, so carefully nurtured by her mother and her grandma, had turned so completely into *his* disciple, following him about, mimicking him, regarding him worshipfully. He drew the girl close beside him on the wooden bench and held her little wrists up so the tips of her stubby fingers just touched the keys.

"That's the position you want. You'll get more power and mobility that way."

He played the First Prelude and Fugue for her. The veins rose on the backs of his hands as he rapped the keys in crisp staccato. His head vibrated with the trills. His daughter gazed up at him. She had expected no less. She would learn to play it just that way.

He raised his eyes from the keyboard. The French doors opened to the terrace and the soft, damp lights of the buildings surrounding Gramercy Park. He had placed the harpsichord precisely for this vista. Behind him, the dining room with its stalagmites of newspapers, the Rosenthal still in crates, unable to come to rest in a china closet. He'd moved the piano into the dining room too. Now, from the bench at the harpsichord, his view was serene, nostalgic.

He returned home late these nights, putting in long days at his new research lab. He saw patients from eight until two, marching to the flawless routines Doris Needham laid out for him. He marvelled at how fluidly it all ran, how grateful his patients were for the absentminded conversation and the politeness he routinely accorded them, for the erudite allusion he occasionally tossed out.

At two, he took his fifth cup of coffee, black, and drove to the hospital, to the laboratory. *His* laboratory. Four white-coated assistants, a suite of offices, two part-time clerks.

Director of Research. He had never imagined this for himself. But several assiduous months in the library had confirmed that cancer research was eminently fundable. He had left it to Hilda Marks to articulate a project and work up a proposal. Hilda was a meticulous and also an imaginative researcher, but a woman incapable of proposing a project of her own, a woman cowed by the title, "Director." She served the men who craved such titles. Nathan knew he was blessed to have her. She supervised the project each day until he arrived. She brought him lunch and reviewed with him the morning's progress. They worked into the night. At eleven, he drove her home and then headed back to Gramercy Park.

As he moved to the C-minor Fugue, he studied the lights surrounding the little park. They could be stars. He could be one of those winged men of science fiction, zooming toward a star-specked horizon. His lips arched in a faint smile. He had to admit he was surprised to find himself so absorbed in research. It was to have launched his ascent at the hospital but it was proving pleasurable in its own right. Time vanished in the lab. Hilda would call a halt to the day. She was a gem, Hilda. Uninspired in bed, but invaluable in the lab.

He wished his father had lived to see the lab. It was almost a year ago, in that oblivious, benumbed week before the New Year, when calendars are too laden to accomodate unexpected events. Nathan had quoted Marcus Aurelius in the eulogy. Irv had almost embraced him. They had faced each other and nodded significantly, each grasping the other's elbows firmly in his palm.

He skipped ahead to the A-major Prelude. His father had nothing but scorn for his accomplishments at the harpsichord and had very little comment about Carla or about the Weisenthals. He did not appear to take much pleasure in Alexandra, either. Not as much as in Irv's children. But the research grant, the lab with its white-coated little army under Nathan's command—this, Nathan was certain, would have won his father's admiration.

"Tomorrow," he told his daughter, "your harpsichord lessons begin in earnest. We'll be very busy, sweetheart. I'm going to take you skiing this weekend and teach you to play the C-major Prelude, too. So you'd better get a good rest."

Years later, he would be asked if he had ever missed having a son. He would reply that he had never considered the question. Alexandra remained a steadfast disciple.

February is a month of artifice and convention. Days anointed as feast days by the polity solely to keep its members from going mad with unfulfilled yearning. The ancients, who felt more keenly the authentic pulse of the Earth, saved their festivities for times of harvest, rekindling, and resurrection. February is a month of desperate quiescence when only the dauntless remain hopeful, and only the most restive stir. It is the month that Lily's husband Howard hanged himself.

"I'm terribly sorry, Lily," Nathan said when he got there. He detested madness. He froze within her slack embrace.

"Did you hear he left a note?"

He wished he had called instead of rushing over.

"Lily, I want you to know that I'd be honored to deliver the eulogy," he said.

"It'll be a cremation," she said. "No speeches. But thank you for offering, Nathan. Howard left a note."

Lily was small, crumpled, translucent. She sat on the leather couch where Howard's patients had conjured their dreams.

"I have known for some years that I am not alive," she read. "By that I mean I am incapable of love. With you, Lily, I have grown increasingly aware of my terrible deficiency. You mourned the death of our son while I rummaged through classical texts on the meaning of death. I watched you grieve and then heal while my own threadbare emotion remained a pale monotonous whine. You have healed because you can love. You are concerned for your patients. I am contemptuous of mine. You even love that poor stupid retriever of ours. I am ashes and always have been."

Lily searched for Nathan's eyes but they were elsewhere. "So that's it," she said. "Howard had no delusions."

Nathan knew immediately that he must leave. "Lily, dear, if there's anything we can do, never hesitate to call. You know Carla thinks you're wonderful. So if there's anything we can do . . ."

Carla had chosen powder blue for their bedroom. Phil Neuman's favorite shade. With the spread rolled back, her bent knees made two powder blue mountains of blanket. Papers ascatter, files in stacks with markers protruding like tongues. She was compiling a glossy coffee-table book.

He slung his Burberry over a wooden hanger and considered its verticalities. Howard must have looked something like this, he thought. He thrust the hanger into the closet and leaned back heavily on the closet door to seal it shut. But Howard slipped past the jamb and hovered before his eyes. Ashes, he had said. He said he felt like ashes. That he could not love, that he could not grieve. A pale whine, he had said. Nathan wondered if *he* had appropriately mourned when his father died, if he had felt the proper grief. He had delivered an excellent eulogy; everyone said so. He sat at the foot of the bed and untied his shoes.

Carla was riffling through the papers on their bed, arranging them in piles. He wondered what her book was about but could not ask. He knew she had told him once. He wondered what she was like as she went about her day. He imagined her with her hair bound in a bandana, dusting ferociously. But that was ridiculous. Rose, the housekeeper, did that. She was busy, he knew, at the National Arts Club and with the Gramercy Park Association, but he could not say quite how. Friends and colleagues left messages for her. Organizations sent her mail. People warmed to her. Her face shone. She was negotiable and gracious and widely welcomed. He needed her for that alone.

He was no longer dismayed at her unresponsiveness, but proceeded unhurriedly, deliberately. A patient beach-comber with a Geiger counter, each day hoping anew to unearth the elusive gold watch. He wanted above all else to be blameless.

"It's not your fault," she would say.

"But it would make me feel grand," he would say.

"It's fine as it is," she would say.

She laid the stacks of papers on her lamp table, threw off the blanket, and shuffled to the bathroom. She brushed her teeth and returned, waiting under the cover for him to put aside his magazine and flick off his bedlamp.

"Would you agree to having another child?" she asked.

Nathan could not imagine a child other than Alexandra. She defined his fatherhood.

"It's about time for another, I suppose," he said.

"But you must want it," she said.

"Well, yes. Of course," he said. "Of course. Why not? Two seems about right."

The Hale Estate had a rundown tennis court enclosed by vine-covered cyclone fencing. All in all, a very ugly affair. The Szabos hired a man to patch the surface and another to teach them tennis. Tom bought a pile of Lacoste shirts and racquets of various sizes.

"I couldn't tell much by holding them at the store," he explained. He was surprisingly good for a novice. Hard-hitting, fast on his feet. A natural strategist. Nathan suggested a book to improve his form. Tom laughed.

"It's too late for form," he said. "I just want to get the job done. Just want to play well enough to beat you." Once more, a good-natured laugh.

"There's more to the game," Nathan insisted.

"Winning is enough," Tom said.

Tilly's game was hopeless. Eventually, Armand became their regular fourth. Nathan, Carla, Tom, and Armand. Saturday afternoons and Sunday mornings. Zoe read the paper. Tilly put Band-Aids on the children. The Szabos' housekeeper served sandwiches with gin and tonics. In August, Carla retired to the sidelines to sit out her term. The Ackermans went to Maine to visit with Zoe's family. "We could hit a few," Nathan said to Tom. "Not a game, you know. Just hitting." "But I'd like a game, Nathan. It would be good for me if you don't mind," Tom said. Tom lost to Nathan every time. And every time, he laughed and thanked Nathan for putting up with him. Nathan said it was no trouble at all. He was grateful for the use of Tom's court. They played each weekend until the leaves dropped from the vines on the cyclone fence. "It's just not normal," Nathan told Carla. "He loses every time and still keeps coming back. Doesn't seem to care." "He enjoys your friendship," Carla said. "He enjoys the activity. Tom just enjoys *himself*." "Next spring," Nathan told her, "we ought to build our own tennis court. The Szabos are just dabblers, and there they are with a private court. Messy court. They don't even keep it up." I like that scruffy court, Carla thought. It's like Tom. "Next spring," Nathan continued, "we'll build a *real* court down near the lake."

Ten.

"It's Nathan!" Sophie exclaimed, holding up one hand to silence her husband while the other pressed an oversized receiver to her ear. The brown silk insulation on the telephone cord in Prague's Alcron Hotel was frayed. The sound was intermittent. "A girl. Fair, with long legs. Bigger than Alexandra was. Everyone is fine. Oh, *Katte*! I want to go back and see my new granddaughter!" "I am soon finished with the conference here," he reassured her. "What is the name, this new one?"

"It was hard to hear him. So far away. Lee, I think he said. Lee."

"Lisle!" Felix clapped his hands in delight. "They named her for my mother. He must have said Lisle."

In fact, Nathan had said "Emily," but he was very far away. When he met the Weisenthals at the pier, Sophie insisted on being driven directly to Gramercy Park.

"Emily," Carla corrected her father. "It's Emily."

"Lisle-le!" Felix persisted, tickling the sole of the little foot. "So spirited! Beautiful little Lisle!"

Lisle loved everyone and demanded nothing less than absolute adoration from all. Every visitor was hugged and kissed with convincing ardor and confounded by her unabashed seductiveness.

"You're handsome," she told Armand, tugging at her pinafore and thrusting a face into his as incandescent as a ripe peach.

"Oh you say that to all the boys," Armand chided. "I bet you tell your daddy he's handsome too."

"My daddy's very smart," she assured him.

"And you, Miss Goldilocks, could melt a stone," Armand replied.

Alexandra had always been a sort of miniature adult. With Lisle's arrival, the world was suddenly filled with children. She clapped her hands over Nathan's eyes when he tried to read to her from *The Odyssey*. He was forced to yield to her preference for *Madeleine*.

In this buzzing, blooming garden of verses, Carla is a rosebush. They see *Mary Poppins* and the Hunter College Children's Concerts. They visit Santa at Macy's and skate at Rockefeller Center. The girls wear matching dresses and chesterfield coats from Lord and Taylor. Carla tells them about their father's research, so much as she can understand. And about the need to love all God's creatures. She tells them God is the name for the sweetness in all living things. She teaches them the importance of good manners and good grammar and shows them how to put on gloves, pressing the spaces between the fingers of one hand against the spaces of the other hand until each finger is smoothly encased.

On Friday afternoons, she picks them up at the Friends Seminary and drives across town to Fairway Market. She wears oxford shirts and tweed blazers. Her brown curls shine. She is blithe. She reaches out as if through liquid. Lustrous peppers, red and green and orange and yellow, some plump and jolly, some lean and curled as a waxed mustache. Dewy, crisp lettuces: citrine and mulberry. Impudent radish knobs. Crunchy beans wriggling beneath her hand like newly-netted sardines. Escarole, chicory, arugula, watercress, and masche. Fresh-baked loaves, dusty with ochre flour, crackling with sesame, caraway, and bran. Lemon curd. Marmalades. Lekvar and honeyed mustards, all in bevelled glass jars.

Citarella's for fish laid out on beds of cracked ice, gossamer fillets of pink and white and bluish grey. She crushes a sprig of fresh dill in her hand and holds her palm out for her daughters to inhale.

The Henry Hudson Parkway is banked by cherry and apple trees in bloom and new grass the color of May wine. She will cook with wine and herbs and warm the bread. They will moisten their fingers to lift bits of its crust from the table top all through the meal.

Hassah helps unload the car. She, too, inhales the fresh dill. The magnolia has shed her petals and the buds on the weeping cherry have finally burst. Carla is overjoyed to see them. Soon the wisteria will appear at the rear porch rafter and the slope to the lake will become a brothel's parlor of garish gowns and musky perfume.

The children run to the rabbit warren to greet the red-eyed survivors of Nathan's laboratory. Hassah and Sophie try to keep them alive through the week and dispose of their failures before the family comes up from the City. Nathan arrives on Saturdays with a new supply. Lisle nuzzles her

63

face in their straw and their soft white fur. "Mmmmmm," she says.

There are two cats now, the walloping Maine Cooner and a sleek Siamese who arrived mysteriously when Lisle was barely two. "Gustav," she had said, pointing to the shy new cat.

"Silly Lisle thinks 'Gustav' is the word for 'cat,'" Alexandra said.

"She's right in a way," Felix said. "In this house, all cats are named Gustav. Except for me. I am Felix the Cat, eh, Sophie?"

"They can't both be Gustav," Alexandra said gravely. "They'll get confused."

"But no, they won't," Felix explained. "You see, they have different last names, these two Gustavs."

"Oh, Grandpa!" Alexandra was disbelieving.

"Well, just look at them. This huge, round Gustav must be Gustav Mahler, and this delicate, leggy Gustav must be Gustav Klimt."

"Mahler, the real Mahler, was neither huge nor round," Nathan put in.

"No, no that's not the point," Felix insisted. "It's the sound of it. The way the words form in the mouth. 'Mahler' is a huge, round sound. 'Klimt' on the other hand...well, you can see what I mean."

"Actually, Felix, I don't see it at all," Nathan said. "Where do you get all this stuff, anyway?"

"You must listen, Nathan. Rudolf Arnheim says, 'All seagulls are named Emma.' And when you attend to it, you can see that they are. Don't you agree?"

Nathan could not imagine what his father-in-law had in mind. Once again, he thought wistfully, there was some vast chasm that separated him from Felix. It recalled the time the old man had spoken of miracles.

Lisle happily called both cats Gustav. Eventually she was old enough to understand Felix's explanation, and then she did understand it absolutely. She was the only one who understood and Felix knew that and adored her for it.

In this delirium of wisteria and dill, of her daughters' shrieks of delight, of her mother's kisses and Hassah's embraces, of her abundant father and the two Gustavs, Carla was more than compensated for Nathan's late nights and for his absences on Fridays. She relinquished him, she decided, to be forgiven for being an inadequate wife, for disappointing him in bed. She had failed to learn to love him. That he must withdraw was, for her, as universal and immutable a principle as any law of Nature. Her sacrifice was necessary to the balance and order of her world.

Her life was, in every other respect, so overflowing, her joy so complete, that she took no notice of it, never paused to mark it, nor to give thanks for it. Such limpid happiness does wash over us without our noticing. It is the soundless transparency of perfection, of senses and energies thoroughly engaged. The absence of trouble leaves no tracks. Each day stimulates and produces until it exhausts itself. Action and the world are so in tune that there is no consciousness of a self apart from them. We take notice of our lives only when something is amiss, when the engine falters and something is found wanting. When this idyll crumbled, as it had to, Carla would remember her happiness. And that is the only consciousness she could possibly have of such bliss: the memory of it.

Every warped old window of the inside porch had been coaxed open and still the heavy August air lingered, having no better place to go. The white wicker and crisp blue-and-white checkered cloths did their best against the torpid heat. Carla wore a white sundress with straps criss crossing her bronzed shoulder blades and carried a basket to the stretch by the fence where scores of zinnias, crimson, gold, magenta, and pink, thrust their bold, hearty heads toward the sun. Her basket full, she returned to the kitchen to snip their stems and arrange them in sportive bunches throughout the house.

At four, the Perrins and the Szabos arrived for doubles. Carla and Nathan against Tom and Marian. The new clay court was nestled in a pear orchard, sheltered from the winds off the lake. Lew Perrin and Tilly Szabo sat low in the Adirondack chairs at courtside, sipping iced tea. All about them, dark-leafed branches bent with hard green fruit. Lew smiled. The sight of his sweet-natured wife, poised in concentration to receive a serve, clearly pleased him immensely.

"Carla, you're supposed to be covering that side." Nathan was unforgiving. "You let it get right past you. Pay attention, will you? Fifteen all."

But she could not pay attention. Not with that bear so near. The bear was huge that afternoon, and his warm bear-breath engulfed her everywhere. When they were backcourt and he was laughing his gurgling bear laugh, when they were both at net and it was impossible to breathe.

She caught his eye as they each moved to their deuce courts. His shrug was an apology. It meant he knew what he had done. What his presence had done. The heat, the damp-ness were insufferable. Rivulets of sweat ran down to the cuffs of her anklets.

He stayed behind to help her with the glasses and pitcher as the others made their way back to the house. She could smell his damp tennis clothes, sweet and heavy.

"I saw you cutting zinnias when I drove by earlier," he said. "You were just standing there with your basket and that white dress and you know, I thought there were zinnias sprouting from your neck and your shoulders and the bend in your arms. The heat must have gotten to me."

Eleven.

Cancer research is like its subject. One project engen-ders another. Nathan's research ultimately focused upon the transport of lipozomes, a project with far broader applica-tions than ophthalmic cancer. It was, Hilda said, a natural. And so a second proposal was drawn, a second project launched, and a second suite of laboratories inaugurated.

Nathan was peerless. His research brought the hospital more from the NIH than that of any of his predecessors. And there were matching gifts from Harknesses and Sloans. Heaney glowed as he introduced Nathan at hospital dinners. He had a new and larger army of residents under his command. Most evenings he could leave by eight. Mondays, he took Hilda back to her place for a nightcap. Thursdays were for music. Nadia, a Russian emigré he'd met at a conference in White Sulphur Springs, loved opera and chamber music and believed she loved Nathan. Her aristocracy delighted him as much as her devotion. On Fridays, they dined at her apartment on Central Park West and listened to music late into the night. He loved the smooth, hard ivory of her hipbones. The Beethoven E-flat Trumpet Concerto.

"It is said," Nathan told her, "that Beethoven wrote his music for all mankind, but that Bach addressed his music directly to God."

When the music concluded, Nadia rolled over and extended an arm toward the cassette player. The Hafner. "Yes," she said, "and Mozart wrote for the angels."

On Saturdays, he was on the tennis court in Peekskill by nine. His serve was never so strong, so accurate. His ground strokes had a mean topspin. When Nadia grew impatient with the demands of his schedule, she was easily replaced.

A step forward to wait for the moving chair to catch them behind their knees and lift them away. A low whirr punctuated by clicks as the pulley ratchets meshed and then silence white as an empty page. Far below them, brightly colored skiers wiggled past and vanished. A tiny lurch as the mechanism stopped and their chair swayed with the languid rhythm of a drunk discoursing from a lamppost.

"I haven't regretted losing that appointment," Robin Colby was saying. "At the time, though, it felt like the loss of life itself. I loved the feeling of climbing upward. I thought my heartbeat would slow and I'd stop breathing if I ever had to spend my days on a plateau."

"Yes, I know exactly what you mean," Nathan said.

"Being chief would have been a high for awhile but then it would have become another plateau. You think perhaps we need to keep climbing because we can't bear children?" Nathan knew he must have appeared puzzled because Colby began gesturing as if to illustrate his point. "Ascent giving assurance of life ongoing. Do you think we press forward to keep from thinking of death?"

"That's a bit overworked, Robin," Nathan said. The pulley ground to a halt, and then lurched forward again.

"But, you know, creative endeavor lets us sort of give birth over and over. That's why this research grant has meant the world to me," Robin continued.

"You really think of it as giving birth?" Nathan asked.

"It *is* giving birth. Just look at women. Do you think they really care about climbing? Do you think they worry about immortality as we do? That they take all this as seriously as we? Well, they don't. They have children and that does it for them. Happiness is so much easier for them."

They were well above the snow-encrusted hemlocks now.

"Better not let Carla catch you talking like that. She's taking lessons from Alexandra. 'Biological destiny' can get you into deep trouble at our house." They slipped off the lift chair and traversed to the ridge. "You know, it's interesting that you enjoy your research so much," Nathan continued. "I love mine, but I hadn't really considered why."

"Immortality, Nathan. Immortality. Women don't give a damn about it. They have babies and they're as eternal as the earth they stand on. *We* have to press onward and upward. But if we put something in the world that wasn't there before, something enduring like research, it's like having babies. It's better, in fact." He gave a little snort to retrieve the mucus that was beginning to drip from his nostrils. "When I'm in the lab, I give birth every day!"

Nathan was mute. He wondered if the metaphor fit him as well. He was uneasy with Robin's view of women, a view that put them oddly in the ascendancy. An admiration that could almost be envy. It struck Nathan as perverse.

At the base of the mountain, Colby came to a hockey stop, sharp and neat. "You were racing me all the way down," he said, calling to Nathan over his shoulder.

"I don't race," Nathan said. "I attend to form."

"Your form is splendid," Robin said. "But you *were* carving very narrowly to catch up with me. It's just as I was saying. Even in our descent, we strive, we compete. It's our biological program. Women are lucky."

"Just don't get Carla and Alexandra started or I can promise you'll never be invited to dinner again," Nathan said. Colby *does* envy women, he thought, and shuddered.

Now the lift bore them higher up the mountain.

"Are you sure you don't miss being chief?" Nathan asked.

"Never even think about it," Colby said.

Nathan thought about it all the time. Two research projects and he still thought about it all the time.

"Research is enough, then? Really enough?" he asked his colleague.

"Research, the kids, the country house, skiing, women. Yes, it's plenty." They were poised at the ridge now. Colby planted his poles and surveyed the steep, narrow slope below.

"And Reena? You know your wife is something of a paragon at our house. A career woman in the same profession as you, raising three kids and all. Carla and the girls think Reena is 'Woman of the Year.'"

"She's an excellent ophthalmologist and a very good mother but she's not much woman. Not much woman at all." Robin adjusted his goggles.

"C'mon, Robin, that's not fair."

"C'mon, yourself, Nathan. You screw around a lot. Would it ever even cross your mind to screw Reena?"

"Robin, you can go too far, you know." Nathan bent to begin his descent.

"What's the big secret, Nathan? We're both screwing around. Reena knows it. Carla knows it. They're not enough for us. They know that, too, and they don't mind, believe me. They've borne their children and they're happy. We're the ones left craving something more."

"For godsake, Robin!" Nathan planted his poles and pushed off down the mountain.

At dinner at the lodge, Carla proposed a toast to Lisle who had won the junior slalom that afternoon.

"I thought you had to be eight to enter," Colby's young son, Marco, said.

"Yeah," Lisle grinned. "I lied. Anyway, I'm going to be seven very soon."

"Nobody who's eight still has both front teeth out," Marco scowled.

"Well," Lisle retorted, "maybe with my teeth missing they thought I was a very, very old lady."

Amid the laughter that followed, Nathan turned to his little daughter and pressed her glowing cheeks tight between his palms. His nose just grazed the tip of hers.

"Oh Lisle! Lisle! Promise you'll never be a very old lady! Promise you'll never be older than seven!"

"My God, Nathan!" Carla looked away quickly to keep from making too much of it.

But Nathan held his little daughter close to his side. "Seven is a wonderful age," he said. "I will be seven with you. We can both be seven forever!"

Hilda had left hours ago. It was probably four in the morning. He strode through his laboratories, letting his fingers graze the cold black stone benchtops. They were extensions of him, they were *of* him. He extended as far as the walls. Beyond, perhaps. From his office, Bach's B-minor Mass poured forth, coating the benches, the incubators, even the rabbits in their covered cages, with its haunting, seraphic sound. Mount Sinai Hospital wanted him to bring his projects there. They could make him chief in three years, when Don Drazen retired. *"Gloria! Gloria!"* He would have a chat with Heaney. Heaney would make a counterbid. He was in play. *"Glo-o-o-oh-r-i-a!"* Director of research, full professor, chief! He stood in the doorway to his office and turned to behold his laboratories once again. A glass stirring rod stood in a beaker nearby. He took it between his thumb and his forefinger. It was his baton. Yes, he thought. Yes, it's happening. Yes! He would soon have his pilot's license. And his shiny new Cessna Skyhawk. He could already feel the engine whirring within him. He would fly, actually fly!

"*In Excelsis Deo!*" He was conducting a chorus of a hundred voices accompanied by full orchestra. Behind him, the Schnitger organ opened its immense throat and poured lush arpeggios through the labs. He turned to the organ and, pressing his left palm slowly toward the heavens, commanded the organmeister to give all his strength, his breath, his very life to his instrument. "Bach," he shouted to the organmeister, "addressed his music directly to God!"

"*Aaaaaaaaaaaah! Aaaaaaah!*" The chorus attended to his every movement, their eyes fixed reverently upon the forceful strokes of his baton and the fierce uplifts of his palm.

"*In Excelsis Deo!*" Mouths stretched to their limits and the swell of voices resonated through the labs. His knees pumped. Up. Down. His chest heaved. Perspiration dripped from his brow. His arms wove rapturous arcs through the air. The chorus ended. Exhausted, sweating, he dropped his chin to his chest. His arms fell limp at his sides. The glass baton splintered on the floor. He let himself fall forward against the lab bench. He shuddered. The firm swell in his trousers endured. The wetness had soaked through and was already growing cold.

PART TWO

Twelve.

July. Days of light. Days of unremitting cheerfulness. Nights like days. A time of light unceasing.

Fifty. He had said the word over and over in the last two years in order to locate it properly in his mouth. "I am close to fifty," he would say. "I am, believe it or not, approaching fifty."

It should toll a halfway point, he thought. As a half dollar. A half century. But surely he did not expect to live a hundred years. It was, then, not at all what it should be. It was more than halfway. Much more. When had he passed midpoint? How had it slipped by him? He was said to be at "midlife" but that word now seemed a cruel euphemism for something much nearer to the end than to the beginning. Or was the line beyond this point somehow curved or irregular? In any event, the measure of time that took his fiftieth year as "midlife" was no Euclidean measure, he was certain of that.

How he craved in winter the sunlight and laughter of July! Yet, the seventh month came freighted with cloying sunshine and laughter reverberating in its heat as in a nightmare.

He had become someone. He had a name, a reputation. He had a family: A nest of daughters and in-laws wove itself about him. He had the society of both colleagues and friends. He had cultivated his interests and developed his talents. His eldest daughter played duets with him on the harpsichord; his youngest matched him curve for curve on the ski slopes. They used his words, his phrases in their conversation. He was well-exercised and perpetually tan. His was unquestionably the good life. There was nothing to want but to repeat it, to live it exactly that way yet another day. Days of incessant sunlight.

He might have mastered the oboe or the viola. He might have chosen architecture. An academic life perhaps. Or the law. He might have taken up photography. Or golf. He had never learned to speak Italian. Had he settled in Europe after the war, married the German woman with whom he'd passed such delightful times . . . That would have been another life entirely. He would not design a museum nor teach Shakespeare. He would remain a man confounded by cameras. He would speak French to the Italians. He was who he was. Alternatives stood now like markers along a way that was already behind him. They were the names of what might have been and they were cold, granitic. He was precluded. He wondered when that had occurred. Ten years ago he had learned to fly a plane. Anything was possible then. This good life had congealed about him. There was nothing now but the repeating. Nights like days. A time of light unceasing.

"I would call it Manneristic," the woman was saying. She wore a dark green dress so unfashionable it was endearing. A youthful bosom rose above the scooped neckline. Some sort of rayon that had been to the dry cleaners too often. More than fills the hand is wasted, Nathan mused, contemplating the freckled mounds. He'd been pacing impatiently about the icy auditorium lobby, picking out bits of conversation, waiting for the concert to resume.

Four muted notes on a xylophone. On a steamer, they might have signaled lunch. Nathan returned to his seat. A warm July night is not a night for "Die Kindertodenlieder," he thought. The contralto was terrible. July is no time for children to die, he decided. He rose to leave just as the pianist reappeared onstage.

His car slid indifferently down the Rockefeller University driveway and onto East End Avenue. He would thank Marvin Lampert for the ticket and say it had been a first-rate concert.

The damp July heat threw gelatinous halos about the streetlamps surrounding Gramercy Park. He paced the tiny terrace where beads of rain dotted the pink impatiens and glanced at the clock tower rising to the south of the Park. It was Friday. Carla was in Peekskill. He would not join her there on Friday, even if it meant dining alone. It was their arrangement, a symbolic renunciation by which they signalled to each other what their marriage had become. And now there was the business with Tom. Tom Szabo might be. . . well, interested in his wife. Interested. He wouldn't be fucking her. Well, Tom could be doing anything. But Carla—that's what he meant about it—Carla could not be fucking Tom. It was enough for her to give in to *him* occasionally. Carla had no interest in sex. Otherwise, she was an excellent woman. She would be shocked if Tom. . . It was a flirtation. Women were like that nearing forty.

The baroquery on the buildings to the south of the Park grew indistinct in the dampness. Tom would never risk it. They were tennis partners. He advised Tom on new patents. They spent vacations together. Tom had his pick of women. He wouldn't make a serious pass at Carla. They were flirting, that's all. The clock to the south of the Park said five past eleven. He would be up for most of the night, he knew.

The woman in the dark green dress had had a tiny hook at the end of her nose and keen dark eyes that flashed intelligence. A sparrow of a woman. Manneristic. What had she been speaking of? Not Mahler, surely. He was uneasy. He could not really say what Mannerism was. She had known when she used the word, but he could not have answered her had she been speaking to him. He left the terrace. Hegel's Philosophy of Fine Art, he remembered, was where he'd first seen that term. The bottom shelves in their bedroom held the books he'd saved since college. It was Hegel who had made something important of Mannerism. He would find the book.

Yes, it was Hegel. Art history as the history of Spirit made manifest to the senses, the evolution of human ideals incarnate. He'd loved Hegel's analysis of the development of styles. A style, defined by its particular view of the world, moves from its primitive statement to its classic, most perfect statement and then, yes, to its manneristic form and finally to its baroque phase. The primitive expression of an idea occurs when it is struggling to define itself, when lines drawn or constructed in steel or in melody reveal a still inchoate idea in a necessarily abstract form. And then the classic, the most perfectly realized, statement of the idea, the fleeting moment when even the artist himself is not aware of what he has achieved. And from there, decline. For after the classic manifestation of a style, its artists become self-conscious, their work affected, precious, overworked. Manneristic. As when Impressionism degenerated into Pointillism, he thought. And then, further decline to that moment just before abandonment of the ideal: death throes, the baroque phase of the style. An elaboration of a style that carries its forms to excess, that creates a longing for its opposite, that lays the ground for revolution and a wholly fresh idea of the world. What had she been talking about, the woman in the green dress, when she had used the word, "Manneristic?"

They were having supper in the kitchen. After eighteen years, it was still alien domain to him and on this evening, it seemed almost eerie. Carla moved about, pulling forks and spoons from drawers he never touched, producing paprika from the dark recesses of closets he never opened. Corned beef and a cranberry mold.

"Unusual," he told her. "Unusual, but it works." he said.

They were in town for the weekend. Lily's daughter's bat mitzvah. Alexandra would wear her first high heels.

"Carla," he said softly when the girls had left the table, "there's something I must tell you. I've thought about it all day and I'm still not sure how to begin."

She sat opposite, stirring sugar into her coffee. Sugar that had long since dissolved.

"Sweetheart," he smiled gently. "It's not what you think."

"Well, then?"

"It's Phil Neuman," he said. "Your old boyfriend."

She laid her spoon in the saucer and began sipping her coffee.

"Well, he's applied to join the Eye Clinic," he said.

"I didn't know he was an ophthalmologist."

"I thought you knew."

"I only knew he'd joined the navy after medical school."

"Look, Carla. . . ."

"Yes, Nathan, what is it?"

"He came to the department meeting today, to be interviewed." The words were tumbling out now despite his effort to keep an even tone. "He's all swollen, Carla. His face, his fingers, and . . . well, his chest."

"Is he sick?"

"I'll say he's sick!" Nathan heard his voice rise. "He's had electrolysis, Carla! He's on estrogen! He's growing fucking breasts!"

"What do you mean? How do you know?"

"Everyone at the interview knew. We can't admit him to practice with us! He's having a goddamn sex-change operation! They'll cut off his penis, for chrissake! Who does he think he is, applying to practice at the clinic like that!"

Nathan's voice had reached a screeching high note and he found that he was trembling. He composed himself and looked up to meet her eyes. She had left the table and was standing with her back to him. He noticed her broad shoulders heaving under the little collar of dark hair. She might have married Phil Neuman.

"I'm sorry, sweetheart. But I really had to tell you." He rose and walked across the kitchen and put his arms around her. All at once, he felt immense pity for her. She had, he suddenly understood, been as much an exile in that kitchen as he.

"You know," she said to him later, tugging at the frayed blue satin trim on their bed blanket, "you really didn't have to tell me. But it's a good thing you did. Poor Philip. So much pain!"

"Yes," Nathan said, "it's an extremely complicated surgery."

"I didn't mean the surgery," she said. "What he must have been going through all those years! And I could never help him. I just never understood. It's a good thing you told me, Nathan. A very good thing that I can finally understand."

Thirteen.

Small, greyish knots of music lovers at intermission. Straight-backed figures, chins tucked in, chatting and nodding affably. Men in shapeless tweeds, their arms folded across their chests. Rouged women draped in shawls. Thin, sallow girls straight and flat as soda crackers. Bespectacled young men in four shades of black. They drew their glasses of white wine to their lips. Their gestures were animated as they spoke and yet the lobby where they stood seemed soundless.

She was there as he had hoped she would be. The question was how to approach her. She excused herself to her colleagues and moved toward the restrooms. He followed her and waited, a paper cup filled to the brim with ice water in his hand.

"Oh, I'm terribly sorry," she said.

"Please don't apologize," he said, producing a handkerchief. "It's you that got wet." He handed her the handkerchief after just the slightest hesitation. She had smallish breasts, he knew, under the navy-and-white polka-dotted organdy. And they were freckled, he knew. It seemed too much to know this as he handed her the cloth. She dabbed at moisture that had already soaked through. To her freckles, he thought.

"Dr. Kline," he said extending a hand and bowing slightly. "Nathan Kline. I believe I saw you at the Rockefeller concert several weeks ago. We weren't introduced, of course, but I know I saw you there."

"Muriel Berger," she said. "Was that the Mahler?" There was a gap in her front teeth. Passion, he thought.

"Yes, it was," he replied.

"It was pretty awful, I thought," she said.

"Actually," he chuckled, "I left halfway through."

"After we were seated," she said. "You got up and left as the pianist was entering."

"Oh God, you saw me."

"Well, it's more noticeable in small halls like Rockefeller. And in subscribed concerts where everyone knows everyone."

"Well, now you've caught me in two clumsy situations." He paused to catch her gaze. "I'd be grateful if you'd allow me to offer you some dessert after the concert. Your friends, too, if you wish. I imagine you've come with friends this evening?"

He crossed and recrossed his legs as the violinist tore into the Bach A-major concerto. Where would he take her for dessert? Someplace memorable. He could think of nothing. Polka dots. Freckles.

They joined a long queue of concert-goers at Eclair.

He learned that she lived alone, had never married. She was thirty-five. She immersed herself in her work and lived entirely for that. She was a pianist. "Small concert engagements," she said. "Chamber groups and such."

"My God," he said. "You really must have loved my leaving as the accompanist entered at the Mahler concert."

"Hated it," she said.

"Do you ever do solo concerts?"

"Some."

"Chopin," he said.

"Liszt, Rachmaninoff, Mahler," she said.

"Aren't you a bit frail to play Lizst?"

"I stand up to play Liszt," she said.

He could not wait to have her. He ordered a second cup of coffee, a second Riga torte, a second glass of water to wash it down.

"Did you enjoy the violinist tonight?" she asked.

"Ah, yes." He had forgotten the violinist.

"I love the A-major concerto," she said.

"A most intriguing composition," he said. As one suddenly wakened from a nap, he found his thoughts would not arrange themselves quickly enough. And then at last he said, "So ingenious the way Bach weaves the theme of the second movement back into the coda."

"Yes, it's wonderful," she said without hesitation.

"Have you ever heard Wolfgang Schniederhan play it? He's not well known in the States, but . . ."

"Yes, absolutely. He does one of the most interesting interpretations," she nodded.

Nathan's pulse raced. He had never before met a woman so utterly absorbed in her vocation. Consumed by it. Consumed by music which, he reflected, consumes like nothing else. Inflamed by the most stirring music of all. By Liszt! Liszt! This tiny bundle of dainty bones stands at the piano to play Liszt! He imagined standing behind her as she played. Did she have freckles down her back?

"How did you happen to recognize me?" she was saying.

"Actually," he smiled shyly, "it's rather strange. I overheard you using a word I hadn't heard in such a long time. It was the word that caught me. Manneristic."

"What was I saying?"

"I don't know. I can't imagine you were talking about Mahler."

"No, I'm sure not. I wonder what I was saying. It's an important word."

Returning to Gramercy Park, he thought he would invite Marvin Lampert and his wife to dinner. It was Lampert who had provided the ticket to the Rockefeller concert and, many years earlier, the analysis of the A-major concerto. She had taken that analysis for granted. He really must have her.

As the elevator reached the twelfth floor, strains of Purcell's G-major Harpsichord Suite wafted from the apartment. Alexandra was a joy to him these days. She was precocious, and hadn't many friends. Her deliverance was her classmate, Martin, a musical prodigy. His constancy would buffer her through a difficult adolescence. And, of course, her father would be her refuge as she would be his.

He had come to describe the condition of their apartment as scandalous. The dining room was an impenetrable forest of cartons and magazines stacked above eye level. There was no sitting at the dining table or at the piano for the stacks of newspapers, boxes, catalogs and such that were stashed beneath. The kitchen counters had become a grimy colony of tiny boxes and canisters, homes to ancient cinnamon sticks and bay leaves turned brown. His closet overflowed with shoes and jackets Carla had worn in college; there was barely room for his own clothing. And now there were cartons under his harpsichord!

"Carla," he bellowed. "I've reached the end of my rope. I've tried to understand this as a symptom. But now I am telling you to take your boxes out of the living room because I'm certain I will kill you if this spreads any further. Dammit, Carla, get yourself some help, will you?"

"Mom's not home," Alexandra said. "It's her sculpture. She's bringing it to the Y on Friday for the student show. It's just here for the next two days."

"I'm sorry, Alex. I didn't mean to upset you."

"No, Daddy. You're right. She needs help. She'll never get any, though."

He settled himself on the terrace with a bottle of Stolichnaya and a bucket of ice. His daughter's rendition of Purcell consoled him. A sudden August squall had cooled the air but it was warming again and there were no stars. Fear? Rage? Grief? What was it that made his wife hold onto things so? What had happened to her in Prague or in England? How could he have known her, lived with her, all these years and not know the answers to these questions?

He laughed a short, cold laugh. All these years. She had belonged to Phil Neuman all these years. In *his* kitchen, in *his* bed, beside him in his Cessna, it was Phil she had been thinking of. What puzzled him was that the news he'd brought her had not wrecked it. She was saddened, but not by a sense of loss so much as by the knowledge of Phil's agony. It astounded him that Phil Neuman's incipient transformation into a woman had not in any way affected her love for him. "He's the same person," she had explained, "and now I understand him."

Nathan could not understand.

"Am I a stodgy old man?" he asked Alexandra.

83

"You're a mandarin and an M.C.P. but I wouldn't call you stodgy," she told him.

"You know that 'Male-Chauvinist-Pig' thing is silly, Alex. Feminism is a dangerous fad, my sweet. If you ever try to defy your biologic imperatives, you'll find out." He wrapped his arm under her chin in a wrestler's hold and bent to kiss her frizzy head. "But I'll adore you anyway," he said. She glanced up at him mischievously and broke into the *Maple Leaf Rag*.

He returned to the terrace and the Stolichnaya. A mandarin and a male chauvinist pig, he thought. Perhaps he had married too late, had children too late. Perhaps he had become his father after all. His jaw tightened.

He had passed his midpoint. He was in his . . .his . . . Manneristic period. It was true, he thought. Not a very nice characterization, but an accurate one.

"*Veritas*," he said, sinking another ice cube in his tumbler. He had become who he was some time ago, some time that had gone unmarked and unnoticed. And now he was an overelaboration of himself: studied, hyper-refined, excessively mannered.

"I'm an overstatement of myself," he announced to the lilliputian figures on the pavement below the terrace. He wished the stars were visible. Visible, and available for conversation.

Fourteen.

"As Titian was mixing rose madder,
His model posed nude on a ladder.
Her position to Titian
Suggested coition
So he swarmed up the ladder and had 'er.

"I love that 'swarmed,' don't you?" Nathan was grinning and shoveling a mound of goat cheese onto a wheat thin. Marvin Lampert had brought a stunning wife to dinner and Nathan had managed to get Stew and Maxene Abrams and the Perrins as well.

"A Columbia College reunion," Carla said, cheerily welcoming Marian Perrin with a kiss. "Nathan is reading from his collection of limericks. I'm compiling a book and Nathan insists I use his favorites. You know how he manages to take over."

"A good limerick is a good limerick," Nathan said. "How can you omit one that scans in four languages?"

He held an old notebook at arm's length:

> "There was a young plumber of Leigh
> Who was plumbing a girl by the sea
> She said, 'Stop your plumbing,
> There's somebody coming!'
> Said the plumber, still plumbing, 'It's me!'

"Pretty ordinary, but *entendez*:

> "Il y avait un plombier, Francois
> Qui plombait sa femme dans le Bois
> Dit-elle, 'Arretez!
> J'entends quelqu'un venait.'
> Dit le plombier, en plombant, 'C'est moi!'

"And in Latin," Nathan continued.

> "Prope mare erat tubulator
> Qui virginem ingrediebatur.
> Dessine ingressus
> Addivi progressus:
> Est mihi inquit tubulator."

"What about German?" Marvin Lampert wanted to know. "It would have to work in German, too."

"Well, of course," Nathan agreed. "I *did* say four languages:

85

"Es giebt ein Arbeiter von Tinz,
Er schlaft mit ein madel von Linz.
Sie sagt, 'Halt sein' plummen,
Ich hore Mann kommen.'
'Jacht, jacht,' sagt der Plummer, 'Ich binz.'"

Never before had Nathan addressed a domiciliary concern with the attentiveness and energy he summoned for clearing the dining room at Gramercy Park. Now, the long table was drenched in creamy white Rosenthal china. It was what he had so long imagined and hoped for. Perhaps, he thought, he should long ago have applied himself to household matters. He shuddered. The piano at the far end of the dining room seemed a bit spindly, cobwebbish, with the space beneath it freed of clutter.

October wines. Cornish game hens. Slippery slivers of zucchini. Crusty rolls from Veniero's. Carla did this sort of thing very well, he reflected.

"Splendid dinner, Carla," he told her as she paused beside him, lifting his bread and butter dish onto his dinner plate to clear them away.

"Yes, Carla, splendid," they all agreed.

"You could do this professionally," Stew Abrams said.

"Carla doesn't do anything professionally," Nathan said.

"That's not fair," Marian put in. "She sculpts and she's edited several books. This limerick book sounds terrific."

"She's only compiling it," Nathan said. "Part-time. She does everything part-time with no real commitment to anything." He looked up from his plate. Hadn't there been a tiny sparrow of a woman standing at the piano?

Carla returned to the table with a tray of cups and saucers and the coffee service, regal as the Horse of Silene. She kept her head bent to the table, attending excessively to serving.

"Such magnificent china!" Maxene Abrams exclaimed.

"Nathan brought it back from Germany, from the navy," Carla said. "It was my wedding present."

"Ninety-six pieces plus servers," Nathan said. "Carried it up to our first apartment one crate at a time. Remember that little walk-up we had?"

"It's the most sumptuous china I've ever seen," Maxene said. "What a marvelous present."

"Nathan didn't even know me when he bought it," Carla said.

"I picked Carla to match the china," Nathan said.

"You must have felt flattered," Maxene said to Carla.

"She didn't feel at all flattered," Nathan put in. "She felt cheated."

"I would have felt flattered," Maxene said.

"Perhaps I should have married you," Nathan said.

"Nathan!" Maxene said, turning away from him. But the toe of her shoe remained pressed against his.

"I think Carla is just grand," Marian Perrin said, raising her wineglass. "To our hostess, whose talents extend to editing and sculpting and raising two lovely daughters. A truly well-rounded woman! Thank you for this exceptional dinner!"

"I'll drink to that," Marvin Lampert said.

There were tiny babas swimming in thick syrup laced with peach brandy. Carla set them aflame.

"Perhaps you *should* do catering," Nathan said as she set a plate of babas and vanilla ice cream before him.

"I'm just fine as I am," she said, and moved on to Maxene.

"But you have no serious endeavor," Nathan said. "No burning passion."

"Why does she need a burning passion?" Lew Perrin said. "Running a household and raising children is pretty serious stuff. Not everyone needs to rage and burn. Women do things differently, I think."

"A woman helps run your business," Marian reminded him sweetly.

"Actually she created my business," Lew said, closing his hand over Marian's. "If not for her flare for Tibetan primitives, I'd still be in the jewelry business," he told them.

87

"But is it passion that drives her?" Nathan demanded to know.

"Hey," Lew said, "she's my partner. We work together and neither one of us burns with passion. It's not art, after all. It's business. What's all this about passion, anyway?"

There _was_ a tiny woman at the piano. Standing at the piano. And Nathan could see that she wore polka dots.

"But Carla really is talented," he said. "She could run a catering business. She could do much more in publishing. She could sculpt more seriously. With passion. She had a show last month, you know. Everyone wanted to buy her things but she refused to sell them. Can't let go of them. She won't let herself really be a sculptress."

"It's okay to call a woman a _sculptor_," Carla said.

"A sculptor is serious about his work," Nathan said.

"I do it for the fun of it," she said. "The studio at the Y is a supportive, social place. It's not as if I needed the money."

"You don't take yourself seriously. And you can't ever let go of anything! I'm not sure of the connection, but those two things are related somehow." Nathan looked hard into his coffee cup, struggling to ignore the freckled back of the lady at the piano.

"_I_ would love to see the view from the terrace," Marian Perrin said brightly. She stood up and led her husband from the table. Stew Abrams and the Lamperts followed. Maxene remained to help clear the dishes.

"Nathan must have had too much wine," she said to Carla. Her English accent had not faded at all in the years she'd been married to Stew. "Don't let him get to you with all that. You're a wonderful hostess and an even better mother. You're also very good with clay, I think." She stacked the cream-colored plates on the kitchen counter. "This china is undoubtedly the most marvelous ever," she said.

It seemed Maxene's accent had become suddenly grating. "Maxene," Carla said, "please join the others. I'd really rather do this myself."

Carla was a fetal lump beneath the covers. The rose-printed nightgown enclosed her and kept her safe. She would fall to her sleep safely, amid roses. "I'm sorry, Carla. I don't know what got into me." She pulled her sturdy Slavic calves in tight against her thighs and tugged at the thin cotton gown. The efficacy of delicate barriers.

"I shouldn't have said those things in front of everyone," he said. "Really, sweetheart, I'm truly very sorry." The umber curls were buried deep in the blue blanket.

"I just know that if you'd put some passion into it, you could be really terrific at something. You could do something important. Give birth to a dancing star, as Zarathustra said."

"I gave birth to your daughters, Nathan," she murmured. "And I've worked ever since to raise them. It's my biological destiny, remember?" The blanket rose and fell with her breath and she pulled it tightly across her shoulders. "I just don't understand what you want from me," she said.

Nathan stared at the ceiling. Lighted building tops to the south of the Park threw muted angular shapes across it. It's still quite light outside, he thought. The City is very much awake. In the Russian Tea Room, they are drinking vodka in their coffee and in the cavernous apartments of the Upper West Side, musicians are playing their music for each other.

He rose from their bed and walked to the kitchen. A telephone hung on the wall.

"Yes," Muriel said. There was a place on Broadway between Eighty-second and Eighty-third. A little coffee shop on the west side of the street. In a half hour. Yes, she said. She would be there. She would love to. She would.

Fifteen.

November again. Pungent oak and wild cherry leaching into the Peekskill soil. Geraniums unpotted and upended in the cellar. A time for taking in the last of things.

Sophie and Felix put off migrating south until after Thanksgiving and, it seemed, the meandrous, sleeping hound of a house chilled early this year. Felix piled on three warm sweaters and still he could button his old corduroy jacket over them all. He had become smaller.

Gustav Mahler, the Coon cat, no longer slept atop the piano, but contented himself with a more accessible spot under Hassah's bed. Gustav Klimt, the Siamese, had long ago run off and been replaced by a pair of common grey cats. Felix unhesitatingly named them Kokoschka and Gropius, although he would not explain how those names were suggested by their very ordinary shapes. He only left the house for short walks. To the edge of the lake where his eyes became lost in the softly lapping water.

Sophie and Carla drew springy strokes with their leaf rakes, forming mounds of wet brown leaves in the pear orchard. Their efforts made them perspire, even in the cold air, and they could not spare their breath for conversation. They dragged a tarpaulin loaded with the last leaves to the road's edge just as the sky turned that November shade of lavender splashed with vermillion.

"I'm losing the girls," Carla told her mother when they were seated in the kitchen, warming their hands around mugs of hot coffee. "Alexandra has always been Nathan's. She's never wanted much to do with me."

"She's very much Nathan's child," Sophie agreed, "but she will soon become a woman and then she will come to you, you'll see."

"You and I have always been so close, Mother. I expected the same with my girls, but it isn't happening."

"You were special, *liebchen*. You were our only child and we were fleeing the war. It was an extraordinary time.

90

Don't envy me that time. You have two daughters, twice the love."

"No," Carla said, "it's not working out that way. Lisle has always gone her own way. I find small bits of myself and a lot of Nathan in Alexandra, but we learn about the world outside from Lisle. It's as if she came from some other family."

"She's a wonderful artist," Sophie said. "She gets that from you."

"Her art is nothing like mine," Carla said. "We never talk about it, but I think she looks down on my sculpture. And she never shares her work with me."

"Well, a second child is always more independent. Give it time, Carla. Lisle, too, will be a woman and then she will come to you." She rose and walked around the table to kiss her daughter.

"You're so beautiful. Don't think it's easy for those girls to have such a beautiful mother. But you know, I should put the squash in the oven now."

Carla carried her mug to the sink. It was filled to the brim with cold coffee. "I'll make a salad," she said.

"Will Nathan be here for supper?" Hassah asked, as she laid out the silverware.

"He never comes to the country on Friday," Carla heard her mother say. "He's very busy, Hassah. A very important doctor. He does cancer research, you know."

The worn, chintz-covered chairs were pressed close by the hearth so the grown-ups could suck in its warmth through toes extended almost to the embers. Alexandra, working through a difficult passage of Schumann's *Carnival,* was oblivous to the icy draft blowing off the lake into cracks in the old window frames. Lisle remained at the table, scrawling in her diary. Felix dozed. The women chatted. They'd have departed for their separate rooms by now if not for the hearth.

Carla had always imagined the months of the year laid out in a circle, as on the face of a clock. Perhaps she had seen an illustration in a child's almanac. Perhaps in Prague. November, she imagined at about four or five o'clock. A precarious position, a point in motion toward a resting place at the circle's bottom. November was, she felt, a vagrant time: transitory, fluctuate. There must have been a drawing in a book. In England or in Prague. It was an ancient image, a familiar sensation. The queasy fear that she might slip off the circle at a tangent, out of reach of that centripetal force that held things together. Their smug little huddle about the hearth, for example, could so easily come asunder. She could sense a rumble in the Earth, preparation for a tectonic shift.

A simple telephone call. Nathan would arrive later than usual the next day. But in time for dinner, he said.

Another call short on its heels. Tom. He'd reserved an indoor court for tomorrow afternoon. Armand was free. Could they play doubles? She had to say no. Nathan would not arrive in time. Perhaps he should try the Perrins. Tom was sorry. He would miss her, he said.

And moments later, the telephone again. Tom again. Marian Perrin had had chemotherapy. Leukemia. Just a routine checkup. It must have been a day or so after their dinner party at Gramercy Park. Leukemia. Sweet, ebullient Marian.

Lew made very little sense when Carla called to offer . . . She wasn't sure what she was calling to offer. Perhaps she hadn't made much sense either. The whole thing, she told Sophie, made no sense. She had been right to feel uneasy. It could all come apart so quickly.

Her daughters and her parents went to bed. The embers died in the hearth and the November chill streamed through the old, irregular windows in icy ribbons. She sat hunched at the kitchen table, one hand on the receiver of the telephone. Finally, she dialed the Szabos. It made no sense, she told Tom.

"I'm sorry I upset you," he said.

"It's not your fault," she said.

"I should have told you in person. I know how much you love her," he said. "It was thoughtless of me to tell you on the phone like that. I'm sorry."

"It's okay. I was upset before that. About lots of things, not just Marian."

"I know," he said.

"You do?"

"Yes."

"How do you know?"

"I just do. I can tell."

"It's not you," she insisted. "I'm not upset at you."

"How would you like a nightcap? Or a hug? Or one of each?"

It is sometimes astonishing to discover how destabilized a system can be and yet endure and function. But when it strays so far from its nature as to reach the grotesque, it can blow itself to bits and, in so doing, right itself. Carla had been an obedient daughter all her life and a dutiful wife for almost twenty years. Imperceptibly, over the years, she had strayed from her nature and gone very much awry. So imperceptibly, and so awry that she could not know until his strong bear-arms were tight about her, just how urgent it was that she see Tom that evening.

Saturday morning, the Earth was once more dense and firm beneath her and Carla felt its equilibrium had been restored. The steady hum of the planet, moving in its predictable orbit, hypnotized like the drone of a raga, like the rhythmic gallops of wooden horses on a carousel. Perhaps she was astride such a horse. On a carousel turning so smoothly it seemed to float. Or perhaps it was the horse itself that floated. Through the raucous jubilee of Coney Island, perhaps. Where she'd joined in the laughter, joined in at last, invited by the son of a Hungarian tailor. By a laughing dancing bear of a man from Brooklyn.

Light, composed, she slid through the day shielded from its vicissitudes. She prepared a casserole for the Perrins.

"It can be heated whenever you want it," she told Lew. She rushed forward to hug Marian hard but the sombre frailty of her friend's response subdued her impulse. It was, instead, an ethereal embrace and Marian's smile faded quickly.

"In a few weeks, you'll have forgotten this ever happened," she told Marian, and she returned home.

Hassah crouched on the floor of her room, rocking to and fro as Mediterranean women do in mourning. Her hands were buried deep in the mottled fur of Gustav Mahler. It was some sort of artificial respiration, but the Maine Coon cat could not be roused. Carla wrapped two strong arms about the old housekeeper to still her hands and to catch the torrential outpour of grief.

Mahler was too large, too unwieldy, to lift. Sophie turned up the edges of the Sarouk mat on which he was lying to make it stiffer, more portable. Then Carla and Felix carried it to the pear orchard. Alexandra and Lisle dug deep into the chilled ground. They recited the Twenty-third Psalm and sang "Rock of Ages" and a bit of "Amazing Grace" and Alexandra said the Sh'ma.

Had she been attending to it, Carla would have been surprised to discover that she was not at all enervated by the events of the day. She withstood them with the bland serenity of a pot of warm milk. Had *he* been attending to it, Nathan would have been surprised to discover his wife, rosy and buoyant, inexplicably blithe when he arrived home at the dinner hour.

On Sunday, they made up a doubles game at last: Tom, Armand, Nathan, and Carla. And, without anyone's attending to it, it was quite clear to everyone. The double faults, the reckless lobs. Carla finally excused herself and left. She asked Armand to drive Nathan home. But Armand's knee had given out.

"I'll leave you two to battle it out," he said to Tom and Nathan.

Tom was staring at the grey-green surface and bouncing a tennis ball.

"Were we playing Penn sevens?" he asked.

"Yeah. C'mon, Tom. Winner takes all."

"Nathan, I have to talk to you."

"I don't think that's necessary," Nathan said.

"Look, Nathan, something's happened."

"I'm glad it did," Nathan said.

"No, really, Nathan. I'm sorry. I want to talk about it. I have to tell you that I'm sorry."

"I'm not sorry. I'm glad. She deserves something nice. I gave up trying a long time ago. This is a good thing, Tom. Good for you, good for Carla. Good for all of us."

"Nathan, do you know what you're saying? What are you made of, for chrissake?"

"Rough or smooth?" Nathan asked. "I call rough." He twirled the handle of his racquet and let it drop to the court. "Your serve," he said. "C'mon, Tom. It's your serve."

"Nathan, you're a really sensational guy!" Tom said.

"Serve the ball," Nathan told him.

Sixteen.

Five o'clock in the evening is the finest hour for certain small restaurants. They stand at the ready, laundered and fragrant, bud vases gleaming. They appear empty and still, yet they quiver and tremble like virgin brides. Anticipation is what fills them.

He had left the laboratory early to allow for a leisurely dinner before the concert at Carnegie Hall. Muriel's colleague, Leonid Rosovsky, was the composer whose work would open the program. They would finish the evening at a party in his honor. Nathan congratulated himself for having arranged so early and secluded a dinner.

Her shoulders hunched against the weather as she approached. She was resolute, condensed. She tilted her head back for a kiss. He offered his cheek.

"I suppose I'm a bit nervous in public," he said.

She turned away.

"You want me to kiss you anyway," he said.

"Yes."

"I can't."

They whispered across the spotless tablecloth. Furtive, self-conscious. A busier place, he realized, might have afforded more privacy. But she drew her surroundings in about her like a woman gathering up her evening gown before descending the stairs. Ultimately, he was grateful to be included in the perfect universe that formed about her. Later, at Leonid's party, it would include others: composers, musicians, poets. He would make brief bows and shake their hands.

"Dr. Kline. Very pleased to meet you."

She was a cynosure, a vortex. He feared his envy would betray him. He wanted to announce his connection to her, to vanquish all the others. But he considered that one of them might know a patient of his, one might know someone in Peekskill. You never know. He stayed at the periphery and swooned in his jealousy as if it were lust.

No one could mistake the sickly viridescence in the canvas bubble for sunshine, but it was January, after all, and they drank saccharined beverages and slumped in the Hudson Tennis Club's battered Naugahyde chairs.

"If a Nauga were a real animal, what do you suppose it would look like?" Robin Colby wondered aloud.

"Like you," Tom Szabo responded. "When you're gone, Robin, we'll cover a chair with you."

"No, not with me, you won't." Robin's mouth tightened against his teeth. He adjusted himself in his chair and brought his right hand to rest on a square of white gauze taped to his left arm. He turned to Nathan, who would understand. "Exfoliative dermatitis," he said grimly. *"Periarteritis nodosa.* So, how's that for a happy ending?"

"Are you absolutely certain?" Years of a physician's stoicism flattened Nathan's words.

"Something in my research," Robin said. He was trying to say as little as possible. "I'm on a hefty dose of steroid."

Robin Colby was the victim of perhaps a single drop of protein which had entered his skin and to which he was allergic. The result was that his skin was, quite simply, falling away. In clumps. The bandage covered an area where the deadly antigen reaction had repelled his skin, leaving him to bleed. Steroids, Nathan knew, could retard the reaction or repress it entirely for a time but, once mobilized, immunological templates would persist in forming allergens. Robin would die hideously. His system was determined to reject the research project to which he was devoting his life. Nathan's training sustained him.

"Well, Robin, we must talk further sometime soon," he said blandly. "*You* played especially well today," he said to Armand.

"Surprisingly well, considering," Armand agreed. The melancholic eyes searched the little circle of friends and came to rest on a garish can of sugarless soda. "I'm leaving Zoe," he finally said. "We're getting divorced."

"*That's* no surprise," Robin said. His own acute suffering had exhausted his compassion. Tom put an arm around Armand's shoulders and Armand wept. Nathan thought the greenish glow in the bubble had become suddenly nauseating. He was trapped, panicky. He wanted to be alone with Colby, discussing steroid treatment of exfoliative dermatitis, a thing he knew something about. There had never been a divorce. So much, Nathan thought, is falling apart.

He concentrated on the pragmatics of it. How, for example, to announce a divorce to one's children. How to preserve one's dignity through the obscene mechanics of moving one's summer suits and one's winter suits, one's overcoat and one's shoes out the front door. Does one rummage for old tennis racquets and favorite old cardigans, for boxes of letters and cherished books and then carry them out ceremoniously? Or is it done clandestinely? Or is it all left behind?

He stared at the Formica tabletop. This has nothing to do with me, he concluded. Armand's situation is very different from mine. It was some time before he could rejoin the conversation.

"What will you do now?" he found himself asking Armand.

"Move out, of course. What do you mean, what'll I do?"

"Do you have a girlfriend?" Nathan asked.

"That's hardly the issue," Armand said brusquely.

"There's no one now?" Nathan suddenly realized that Armand might be the only faithful husband among them. Perhaps," he went on, "you should have an affair. It works quite nicely, you know. Divorce is awfully messy."

"Nathan," Armand said wearily, "I think sometimes you should just shut up."

"But you ought to have an affair," Robin agreed, "whether or not you leave Zoe." Colby welcomed this subject, warmed to it immediately. "A woman who is empowering," he said, "and at the proper distance, that's the key thing. You have to keep from knowing her too well. You can't let her shatter your ideal. If you can manage that, it's terrific."

Tom could not enter this conversation. And he could not leave it either. For its duration, he was doomed to shift about in his chair and worry a small hangnail.

"What do you mean, you have to keep from *knowing* her too well?" Nathan was astonished by the naivete in his own voice.

"There's something awful and frightening about knowing anyone really well," Robin said. "Self knowledge, I suppose, is the most terrifying of all. Look inside yourself and what do you find? Ambiguity, continuous metamorphosis. Death is what you find."

"Robin, I know you're very upset just now," Nathan said. But Robin was far too interested in his subject to be stilled.

"Nathan, why are you resisting this? That shadowy stuff, the inconstancy. The absence of anything substantial. Live with yourself long enough and it's all you know. Change, insubstantiality. Death. It's terrifying to be alone with yourself, isn't it?"

"A lot of us like to be alone," Armand said.

"What do you do when you're alone, Armand? Read a book? Plan another business meeting? Pay your bills? That's not looking at yourself, Armand. That's looking away." It seemed Colby would leave each one of them wounded in some way.

"What do *you* do when you're alone?" Armand came back at him.

"I'm the same as you. I can't confront myself either. It scares me sick. But you see, a wife doesn't subdue that fear, Armand. You know her the way you know yourself. You know she has the same defect as you. You need an *idée fixe*. A woman with no ambiguities. Simple. Glossy."

"In other words, you want a bimbo," Tom finally said.

"No, no," Robin said. "I'm talking about not coming near enough to see the ambiguities. A woman close enough to touch, but far enough away to remain exactly as you first conceived her, as you want to conceive her. *She* is comprehendible, unambiguous. She doesn't deviate from your initial solid sense of her. Fucking her gives you a whiff of permanence. Immortality." He stroked the gauze bandage on his arm and tried scratching lightly through it. "Nathan's right, Armand, an affair would do you good."

Nathan looked away. Colby was right about that porosity, that elusiveness, the lack of substantiality. From the day he married her, his wife had confused him. "Tom," he wanted to ask, "does my wife make you feel omnipotent? Does fucking Carla make you forget you're mortal? Does it make you feel like God?"

Tom, he reflected as he headed home on the road along the reservoir, didn't care much for Colby's view of affairs. But of course, Tom had a thoroughbred. Nathan could appreciate Tom's point of view. He knows a good thing when he's got it, Nathan thought.

He paused at the doorstep to the house that swarmed with his in-laws and his children. And Muriel, he thought, Muriel is something solid, concentrated. A substantial *idée fixe*. A laser. Would Muriel come apart somehow if he were married to her? Would her intensity dissipate over time?

Would it be different if he knew she would be with him until he died?

Until he died.

Yes, he thought. She would lose everything then.

Seventeen.

He approached mirrors more cautiously now, taking deep breaths, as if he were about to open a hefty, complicated tome. Something that required pondering. He thought he must have his face pinned up. He had difficulty peering into the microscope. His eyelids should be repaired. Perhaps his chin as well. Tennis, skiing, naps on the terrace: Too much sunshine had exhausted his skin. And there was Colby's skin just dropping away. Armand's marriage and Colby's skin. Dropping away. We should be like reptiles, he thought. A new skin every few years. We could remain in the sun forever.

"Very handsome, Daddy," he heard Alexandra say.

He wondered how long she'd been standing there watching him. She had his pale red hair, his aquiline nose. She was almost the age her mother had been when Nathan first met her. He wished Alexandra looked more like her mother.

"Thank you sweetheart, you're very kind," he said.

"It's true," she said. "You're a good-looking guy."

"And an old one," he said.

"You look your age," she said. "That's not old."

"My eyelids are drooping."

"You're sad," she said.

"No, Alex, that's age, sweetheart."

"You'd look fine if you were happy," she said.

"It all comes together, darling. Age and unhappiness."

She turned away. She was struggling with something. He did not press her but turned back to studying the mirror.

I'll always be thin, he thought. Thank God for that. It was a matter of considerable pride to him that nothing bulged. Not his stomach, not his midriff. He ran on coffee and ate only one meal a day. I'll never have a paunch, he thought.

He liked his hair being grey. It was thick and silky and much straighter than it had been when it was red. Grey hair showed off his tan to advantage, made his eyes bluer. An improvement, he thought wryly. The barber advised him not to shampoo it every day. To save the oils. It made him uncomfortable to arrive in the office with unwashed hair. But he'd been told he'd have his hair a good long time yet. What things to be thinking about!

One of those wished-for summer rains. The sort that get women baking pies. Or, on this surprising day, clearing closets and attics. And cellars.

He had ceased complaining about the *New Yorker*s piled high in the Peekskill cellar, a collection representing twenty-seven years' hoarding. And now, in the tiny downstairs bathroom, his wife stood atop a shaky ladder, papering the ceiling and walls with *New Yorker* covers, slathering the glossy undersides with rubber cement and brushing each onto its place on the sagging walls with a broad wallpaper brush. The aromatic glue had drawn him; his amazement held him there. Scores of magazine covers lay heaped on the floor, arranged by year, theme, color.

"Will you be throwing out what's left?" he asked.

"Well," she said, "there *are* some articles I haven't read yet." Her laughter tinkled. "Yes," she said finally, "it really is time to clear out the cellar. I'll throw out the ones I don't use on the walls."

He wondered how she had come around to sorting through those magazines. She'd had to slay dragons, he knew, to be able to throw them away. He'd never understood about those dragons.

Her dark hair shone like the sprightly magazine covers. She was strong and purposeful. Her voice, her laughter were exhilarated, blithe, unhesitating. Her hands moved deftly among the piles she had sorted out. Kneeling there on the tiled floor, the narrow bathroom tapering over her, she was crouched at the foot of a shaft. He had been there once before. An elevator shaft. An elevator in the wrong building. A gladsome young woman whose voice filled the little space like church bells pealing in a small town. Church bells pealing all at once.

"It's such a charming effect," he told her. "Where did you get the idea?"

"I've been thinking about it for years," she said, not lifting her head from her work.

He imagined her bolted in that bathroom, scanning the walls, planning this little delight. Is that what occupied her in the hours she spent locked in bathrooms? Locked in lavatories around the world, planning an arrangement such as this?

It was about as close in the cluttered bathroom as it had been in that elevator. She was still luscious and vital, he thought. Still a round bowl of ripe fruit. Was she still, or had she become so once again?

Why now? he wondered. She had broken free somehow. It seemed all of a piece. This bold release of the tightly bundled magazines. The lightness of her laughter. The sureness of her gesture. She's in love, he decided.

It was hard to know when Felix's presence in the cavernous second-floor study had yielded to Nathan's. The old man spent shorter and shorter summers in Peekskill, bought no new books, wrote little. His peppery meerschaums grew stale in their rack. Nathan brought boxes of data sheets back from the lab. He bought an audio-cassette player and recklessly accumulated cassette recordings of Bach, Telemann, Vivaldi, and, more recently, Chopin, Lizst, and Mahler. These he intermingled with cassette lectures on recent ophthalmologic research. By degrees, the study became his.

Now he stood at the picture window gazing out at the pear trees, green-caped gnomes, slope-shouldered and rain-wet. There were still abundant reminders of his father-in-law: an oversized phonograph and the heavy black discs that spun on it at seventy-eight rotations per minute. Stacks of psychoanalytic journals in German and Czech. The only other person in the world who actually uses the word "importunate." Veneration had become deference and then a cool but even comradeship. Felix was his comrade. Never the closeness he'd once yearned for: Felix offering him his daughter, Felix cheering him on while he . . . well, that was so long ago. He couldn't have known. Felix couldn't have known. But at the time, it seemed a splendid victory. He thought he had won Felix and had wooed and won his daughter. Won her fairly, he thought. And now she was in love with Tom. He was sure of it. She unbundled magazines stashed in the cellar for twenty-seven years. Ripped off their bindings and tossed them away. Her face was an apple bursting with juice. She was in love, all right, and he envied her.

They lay upon Muriel's bed like herrings. Slim, motionless, glistening. Her skin, he thought, clung too tightly to the bone. She was stark despite the coffee-colored mottlings on her shoulders.

There was so much more he knew about her now. And still, he concluded, still he found her glorious. Some evenings he sat reading and pausing from his reading to watch her at practice. He knew better now the genesis of the rapture that infused her performances.

He had observed her patience and attentiveness, the thoroughly labor-intensive activity that filled her days. He had witnessed her dissolving into it. He had heard her play a minute passage over and over, listening to herself, making fine discriminations between this rendition and that. She was sufficient as her own critic; she never asked his advice. She set her ear for the subtlest expressive distinctions, those meanings that were contained in a fraction of a second. Her medium, he had come to understand, was not merely sound, but time itself. The organization of time was her manner of speaking. The nonchalance or determination in one finger, the tension in a wrist or an elbow constituted her pronunciation. And when it was perfectly right it would be reiterated until it merged flawlessly into a melodic line and then into an entire sonata.

Her long hours at such exercise were the process by which she slipped first her hands and then her arms, her shoulders, and finally the whole of herself into the music her audiences heard. He had witnessed the tedium consuming and then transforming her and he knew that this was the source of what listeners took for the symptoms of ecstasy. He saw now that those sonatas and mazurkas and fantasias were, like peaches in the rusted truck of a small orchardier, the harvest of dedicated dawn-to-dusk labor.

I have seen her offstage, he thought, and yet I adore her. I know what lies behind her spellbinding music, and yet I am spellbound. But he knew that these were still aspects of an ideal. He had not witnessed the craters, the fluctuations and darknesses Robin Colby had referred to in the lounge of the Hudson Tennis Club. She was still as he had first conceived her. An _idée fixe_. He had kept her at the proper distance.

He studied the freckled back she presented. He loved the backs of women lying on their sides, the dramatic rise of their hipbones, the graceful plummet and second climb to the shoulders. That line that defined a cello.

He rose and walked round to the other side of her bed. Not a pretty face. But a space between her teeth. He had known she would be passionate. He studied the fingers poured over the side of the bed. Lean, strong fingers that had been to Moscow. That had flicked and trilled and paused for precisely measured moments on ivory-covered keys in Tel Aviv and Salzburg and Sydney.

He selected a cassette from her drawer and settled himself in the chair beside her bed. Mahler's Fifth Symphony. Fingers that prepared the sweetbreads and frogs' legs he so relished. An extraordinary woman. And at the proper distance. Colby had been right, he decided. She proffered respite and the promise of salvation.

"I love you," he eventually said.

He felt magnified by his words and he said them again. "I love you, Muriel."

He exulted in the sound. He was convinced it might be true.

"I love you," he said once more.

She remained asleep.

Eighteen.

They went to Aspen in October. A time for the trees that give the town its name. Coltish white pickets dashed by tarry scars, splayed against the mountainside without roots or tops. Sometimes a startled branch darting off, breaking the vertical wash of them. And the leaves! Chartreuse and lemon yellow, confusing the sun that lighted upon them.

"Aspen will be ours," he told her. "A shared memory." He was aware that he had begun collecting memories. Like snapshots for one of those albums one rarely opens. He wasn't certain when this had started.

The American Ophthalmology Association's annual conference. He delivered a paper and was applauded at the dinner that followed. She did not attend, but dined with friends, Dieter and Phillipa Schrenk, at their home in Carbondale. It was where they were staying. Away from the others.

He never carried a camera and never much cared for candid photos but before they left, Philippa presented him with a packetful. Sun-dappled faces. Twosomes, foursomes. Grouped about a table, aspens in the background eclipsing them all. Eternal smiles and eyes squinting in the dry, light-drenched air. Muriel laughing and pointing at the little white car, now spattered with red clay, that had carried them through Independence Pass. On the plane back from Denver, he told Muriel to keep the snapshots. And then he was home.

At the office, Doris Needham is superbly starched. Her hair, the lustreless grey of the dead, is tucked into her cap; her face is dusted with unbleached flour. She sets index cards before him and speaks without inflection, her voice just audible above the drone of the air conditioner. She speaks discreetly of his next patient.

"You saw him just last week. He's sure there's a stitch that hasn't been removed. I tried to reassure him. Left eye."

Her energy remains constant throughout the day. She

ushers patients into examining rooms. Artfully moves him to where they are waiting. Her thick crepe soles pad over the old linoleum. Not a step is wasted. He trusts her absolutely. He slips into the washroom and scrubs his hands after each patient. There are wounds on his palm and on the fingers of his left hand. He cannot remember hurting himself. There are occasional sharp pains in his left arm and shoulder. He takes a key from his pocket to unlock the cabinet over the toilet. He swallows some vodka. The days pass.

At the lab, a party to celebrate publication of his research. Hilda has arranged it. He cannot recall when he last made love to her. They have not spoken of it.

"We need to reapply for the grants," she told him when the others were gone. "I can fill out the forms, but I need an outline of the next project. I'll write it up once I have the outline. We'll attach this new publication. That should seal it." Hilda would always deliver. He was a lucky man.

"What is the next project?" he asked her casually.

"That's for you to decide," she said. "January deadline."

"I see." His breath was shallow. He was very tired. "Give me the papers. I'll look them over at home." His mouth was parched.

Flickering, as patterns of light and dark moved across the television screen. Sound turned low, words incomprehensible. A sense of motion in the bedroom. Like a moving train, it kept him focussed on his reading. He hadn't thought about the next project. The paper had taken almost a year to complete. Hilda should have alerted him sooner. How could she expect him to think up a new project just like that? A woman on the television screen. A lady tennis player. He rose from the bed and turned up the volume. Some large-boned woman. Soft, wavy hair. A longish face that benefitted from such hair, he decided. Strong arms, probably Australian. Their women are big, powerful types. Nina Phillips. Some fuss about her wanting to play in the amateur matches. Nathan could not account for the vague vertigo he experienced. The women's matches. That soft, long hair, dipping slightly over the forehead.

"Carla! Get in here! Carla, hurry up!"

"What is it, Nathan? I'm busy."

"Get in here right now! Phil Neuman," he sputtered. "It's Phil Neuman! Nina Phillips is, is Phil Neuman! Look at her! At *him!* For godsake, Carla. He's got a lawyer suing to allow him to play women's tennis. What the hell is he doing?"

Carla stared mutely at the television. Nathan shuffled his papers on the bed. "Look at the muscles on those arms! Is he crazy? He's a goddamn ophthalmologist. He should have his license revoked. Fucking publicity-seeker! It's sickening."

"Be quiet, Nathan. I want to hear this."

"Enough the guy gets himself castrated. Now he's on television suing to play women's tennis! Goddamn idiot! He's trying to ruin the profession."

The news segment concluded. Carla returned to the kitchen. The application forms grew large and soft-edged on the bedcover. Hilda hadn't given him any notes. He didn't have another project. He couldn't possibly think one up so quickly. He couldn't, in fact, think of anything just now. There was no new project and that was that. They would have to continue the present project. He deserved it. After all, his publication had broken new ground. Everyone in Aspen had said so. The NIH could carry him for another three years. He deserved it. Goddamn Phil Neuman. What an asshole!

"I think she should be allowed to play," Alex said at dinner.

"Of course she should," Lisle agreed. "People have the right to change and when they do, they have the same rights as the people they change into. It's simple."

"It's not so simple," Carla said. "But they should let her play. She certainly can't play men's matches."

"So he doesn't play. Big deal," Nathan said. "He's an ophthalmologist, not a tennis pro."

"She," Lisle said. "And Mom is right. She has a right to play."

Nathan left the table. "What a bunch of screwed up women," he said, scooping some papers into a briefcase. "You've screwed up my daughters, Carla. How can you even look at that sicko, much less defend him? The three of you are as sick as he is." He slammed the door behind him.

Lily's office was still beige. Smart and chic and beige. Lily looked especially well. He planted an arid kiss.

"I'm stuck for a project," he told her. "I've put in fifteen years on this. I can't come up with a new project every three years. Who do they think I am?"

"So give it a rest," Lily said. She sat cross-legged in the oversized armchair as she did for hours each day. Nathan darted about, pausing at windows and Ansel Adams prints.

"That's crazy," he said. "Once you get funding, you have to keep it coming. Otherwise they forget you."

"If you don't have another project, what do you want funding *for*?" she asked.

"I have to keep the lab going, Lily. I built that place. It's prestigious for the hospital. And for me. It's what I live for, my life, Lily. It's my whole goddamn life. You know that."

"Time for a new life, Nathan. Get more involved with your patients. Give someone else a chance at research."

"Have you ever thought of redoing this office, Lily? Getting rid of all this beige? Give another color a chance?"

"I had the place redone ten months ago. Beige is what makes me comfortable," she said gently.

"What about *my* comfort?" He was flushed, menacing. "I can't cook up another project just like that! That's what Hilda's for. She's been slacking off," he said. He stood at the window, looking down onto Park Avenue. "Come to think of it, I know why, too." He turned back to face Lily. "Well, she's not paid to fuck me. She's paid to develop my projects."

"I know it's hard to let go of the lab," Lily said, "but you have a reputation now. The most challenging cases are referred to you."

"Practice is not enough, Lily. I told you that years ago."

"Have you thought of why that is?"

"Don't be a goddamn shrink!" he cried. "You're my first cousin and my first love, Lily. Be a pal."

"I'm doing my best," she said. "But sometimes it's just time to move on." She walked over to where he stood and looped her arms about his neck.

"I've got to get going, Lily," he said. "I have to pay a little visit to Hilda Marks." He turned away from his cousin to muffle his words. "That cunt!"

The room he returned to was suddenly unfamiliar. Its walls and furniture were bloated. An unnatural light from the television screen. Phil. Phillips. The frayed blue coverlet pulled back, his papers littering the floor. Ulcerated, edematous, this room. He could scarcely breathe in it. And in his shoulder, a demanding ache.

His wife emerged from the bathroom distracted, remote. She seemed surprised to find him there.

"Will you ever stop locking that door?" he said.

"Please, Nathan. Not now."

"So you *are* upset. You're upset about Phil. I knew it would get to you eventually. You really loved him, I know. But you loved him as a man. This finally got to you, didn't it?"

"It's all right," she said.

"Look, I've never understood you," he said. "And you have never understood me. I think we should get a divorce."

"We can talk about that if you want, but not tonight." Her easy acceptance of that word startled him.

"Are you ever going to replace this bedcover? It's coming apart. I hate this bedcover. And you've always known I hated it," he said.

"I didn't know," she said wearily. "I'll replace it."

"We should get a divorce," he said again. "You're still in love with Phil. You've just realized he's gone. That's why you're crying, isn't it? You've just understood you've lost Phil."

109

"Tom just called." It was a hoarse whisper. "Marian Perrin died this morning. We can talk about this other thing tomorrow. After the funeral."

She turned her back to him and pulled the cover over herself in one round gesture.

"I'm sorry," Nathan said. "That's really terrible." He took a few Percocets for his shoulder. Also a Seconal.

Nineteen.

Years. Years that are a sea of grain. Fine-grained, uneventful years. His daughter's high school graduation. Another research grant. A twenty-fifth wedding anniversary. Inevitable events. Celebrations for which there are protocols; one does not think much about them. Years that run through a sieve.

His eldest daughter is in college. His youngest, exuberant and fiercely creative. His wife leaves their Gramercy Park apartment each morning to shop or to edit books. In the evening, she goes to the Y to sculpt or to a meeting of some sort. He knows she meets her lover on some of these evenings, it does not matter which ones. They might dine at home and then part. He, too, has meetings to attend. Occasionally, they mention divorce. It is a rough strand on a many-wefted loom, a strand never bound off.

The sun continues beating down, its relentless brightness. The world, however, darkens; the same indiscriminate relentlessness.

In Truro, their daughters set out in early morning on bicycles. The sounds of drawers and doors opening; tiptoeing on the stairs; animated, audible whispers. Sounds that linger in the early blue air like fragrance. The rattle of summer morning: all the house is glad for it.

The Szabo children wanted to go along, and eventually Alex and Lisle were persuaded to take the two eldest. They would lunch along the Bay and pedal to Provincetown. The others would meet them at dusk for the dune ride and dinner. Their bikes would be strapped to the station wagon for the ride home in the evening. A summer ritual, the Klines and the Szabos. Dune rides and dinner in P-Town. It was never clear how many bikes were stored in the beach house garage, just as it was never clear how many beds the house actually held. The answer to both questions seemed to be: as many as needed.

Already the second of their ten vacation days. Sand scraping underfoot and sliding about in the bed linen. Stray socks and sneakers wedged under furniture beside puzzle pieces and Scrabble tiles.

The order of meals was forgotten. Tom Szabo settled himself on the deck for breakfast with a plastic bowl of crabmeat salad. He was eating with a soupspoon. Tilly spread peanut butter on damp croissants for the children. Nathan found a fork on the drainboard and dug into the crabmeat with Tom.

"What would be good with this," Tom began, "is some of that spaghetti the kids had last night. I love cold spaghetti." He sucked the runny mayonnaise from his lips. "With tuna fish. I used to eat it that way from my mother's refrigerator when the family was asleep. Cold spaghetti and tuna fish. They counted on me to dispose of leftovers. My father wouldn't look at them. Not that old man."

Nathan remembered his own father had eaten leftovers, had ordered his mother to serve them until every last shred was consumed. "I can't imagine cold spaghetti," he said.

"Oh, Nathan! You missed one of the best things. Tilly, where's that spaghetti from the kids last night?"

"Tom, it was canned spaghetti. It's awful," Tilly protested.

"Better!" Tom said gleefully. "Here Nathan, try this. Only thing is, it should be tuna fish, not crabmeat. Too fancy. Not as good with cold spaghetti as tuna fish."

111

Nathan marvelled at Tom's easy self-acceptance. He remembered Tom in Vail, a novice in a silver lamé skisuit. First, he proclaimed himself "an appalling *nouveau riche*" and then he unabashedly adored that skisuit. And here he was extolling tuna fish.

"Hey, wait a minute!" Tom was ripping open a large white paper bag. It had the familiar orange insignia of Zabar's. "Only my wife would buy prepared tuna salad at a fancy delicatessen on the Upper West Side. Tilly, I can't seem to get it through to you: Tuna fish comes in cans."

"*I* bought the tuna salad," Carla confessed. "I thought it would be easier when we arrived. I know how much you like it."

Tom shot a glance at Nathan. But Nathan seemed not to have heard his wife. He was buried in an old *New York Review of Books.*

"Thanks," Tom said casually. "Sweet of you. Any coffee?"

Nathan noticed Carla pouring more coffee for Tom. He noticed Tom drying the dishes Carla washed. He noticed Carla doing jigsaws with Tom and his kids. He noticed it all. It's all right, he thought. Whatever they want. It's a relief. Tom's a great guy. He wondered if Tilly knew. He supposed not. He fell asleep in the deck chair, head back, mouth agape. The magazine slipped from his lap. Hours later, he roused himself, more drowsy than before, and walked to their bedroom.

Carla was sitting on their bed, her chin resting on her knees. The sun had gotten him, he knew. And the Percocets. He needed liquid. And he had to lie down.

"Move over," he told her. He sounded drunk.

He woke to discover himself scalded. Flesh parched as the bricks of Egypt. Sinuses, eyes, dry as a dune. The scent of dime-store peachblossom steamed from the bathroom. His wife had found an old bottle of bubble bath.

She drew her knees up again when she returned to sit on the bed. This time she was wrapped in a thick white towel.

Peachblossom hung in the air around her and fell to the pillow where he lay. The tips of her fingers and toes were pale on her tanned skin. Mad streams of bathwater crazed her temples. A little clump of bubbles deliquesced on her shoulder.

"Seltzer," he said in reply to her question. "With lots of ice and some lime if we have any."

He propped himself up at the edge of the bed and sipped from the tall glass she'd brought him. Goose prickles rose along his arms. In his eyes and well back into his brain the scratching of fingernails on dry clay pots, insane whispers of desert dying. He plunged his hand into the cold water and drew it across the nape of his neck.

"You look refreshing," he finally said to her.

"Are you okay, Nathan? You want something more to drink?"

He slouched to the dresser and fumbled about for the Bufferin.

"Nathan, something's hurting me," she said. It was the voice of a small child. He wondered when their daughters had sounded so unassuming.

"What is it, Carla?" He was still groggy.

"Something's not right. It's burning. Throbbing, more like."

"What is?"

She kept her chin tucked down as she slowly parted her knees. "I have some vaginal infection or something. Not yeast. I know what that's like. Maybe it's just menopause." She looked up at him, still without raising her chin. Just her eyes, those two aquamarines.

He stood beside the bed now. "Lie down with your knees apart. You know, as if there were stirrups." His fingers probed only a moment.

"Jesus Christ, Carla, you've got herpes! Jesus fucking Christ!" He stood over her, his moist hand poised at a distance from him as if it held a dead rodent.

Her eyes were closed. "Tom never said anything. I wonder if he knows," she said meekly.

113

"Of course he knows. A man can see it. What a jerk! This is your thing, Carla. It's not *my* business." He sat once more at the edge of the bed and held the bedlamp close to her crotch, opening her again.

"Herpes," he said. "The gift that keeps on giving."

"It's no big deal," she said.

"You're really nuts, Carla, you know that? You should hate him for this."

"I love him," she said. She had turned her head and buried it in the pillow. Her shoulders heaved slightly. "I have to forgive him. He's changed my life, given it back to me."

"He's changed your life all right," Nathan said. "And what he's given you is a loathsome disease!"

"I forgive him," she said again.

In the bathroom, he dug his nails into an ancient cake of Lifebouy soap. He brushed his hands, rinsed and washed them again. He expected the soap to sting the cuts on his left palm but it did not. In fact, he felt nothing on that hand. He wanted to puke.

He took a cab to the Provincetown airport. In his brief-case were some papers, a blue oxford shirt, a Dopp kit, and three socks. He got clearance from traffic control and climbed into his Cessna. Still a bit of heat stroke, he thought. But the flight will bring me around.

In two hours, the others would be coming up to Provincetown for the dune rides. Carla would say something about his having an emergency to attend to. He doubted she'd say anything very much to Tom. It was a different thing she felt for Tom, he knew, than he had ever felt for anyone. Than anyone had ever felt for him. It's because of the way Tom is, he thought. He's that kind of guy.

He followed the Atlantic coastline to New York. No moon, no stars. Just the familiar lights of I-95 winding along the coast below and then west toward the river. He continued south, passing the Westchester airport.

It's because of the way Tom is. He wondered if Tom was

114

keeping Carla at the proper distance. They would have to discuss this herpes thing, his wife and Tom would. Pretty soon, they would have to talk about it. It might be hard to keep the proper distance after that.

He would fly under the George Washington Bridge. Just for the hell of it. He could lose his pilot's license. What the hell, he thought. He cut his transponder, dropped to five hundred feet, and upped the engine to a hundred and eighty. The broad Hudson spread out beneath him, a gleaming grey fishbelly, the wide belly of a drugged woman. A tugboat, stolid and snub-nosed, passed to his left. He pulled up the yoke and rose to eleven hundred feet. Back up between the stanchions of the bridge. A loop. A perfect loop. Now, down on the yoke and once again he was under the bridge, taunting the river. Another loop. He was dazed and dangerous. A vacant consciousness at liberty.

Twenty.

"Carla and the girls are still up on the Cape," he told Muriel the next day. "A little contretemps. I was hoping you'd be up for a concert. Something at Alice Tully Hall?"

Sunday in late August the City is evacuated as if threatened by holocaust. Those destined never to escape stare wantonly from doorways and windows. And I, Nathan mused heading north along Broadway, am the one to discover it was all a mistake: There will be no flood, no war, no devastation. Unwitting adventurer, I find this city drained of its roiling contents, now surprisingly pristine and entirely mine. And there was Muriel, perched at the rim of the Lincoln Center fountain, crisply mint green in polished cotton.

"'A consummation devoutly to be wish'd,'" he said, offering his hand to help her down. Her skin was cool.

The rhapsodic cello transported him. Muriel, he thought as he gave himself to the music, was more of a good thing than he had acknowledged lately. He knew he offered less than she wanted and far less than she deserved. Her concert tours, filled with salving productivity, protected her from him. The affection of her audiences and colleagues sustained her. These things stabilized and shielded her. For, in the end, he always abandoned her.

He rose to applaud the musicians. He was immensely grateful for the tiny freckled form that rose beside him. He would take her to dinner at Cafe des Artistes.

"I have to tell you something," she said when they had returned to her apartment. "I'm seeing someone else."

"Why?" he asked after some moments.

"It's been six years, Nathan. You won't leave Carla."

"Who is it?" he asked.

"Leonid. The composer. You met him years ago. Perhaps you've forgotten."

"Leonid?"

"Yes, Leonid Rosovsky."

"Why him?"

"He loves me. He wants us to get married. We have the makings of a very sharable life."

"Do you love *him*?"

"I want to be married."

"Yes, I know. Are you going to put up some coffee?"

"You know I love you," he said when she returned with coffee and cream poured over ice. "And now you've won your point. I really am going to leave Carla."

"I'm not asking you to leave her anymore," she said. "I'm just saying that it's over between us."

The holiday traffic southbound on FDR Drive was more irksome than ever. An accident. A shattered windshield. He would have to move his shoes out of the closets in Peekskill. Carla would take the house, he would keep the apartment. They had spoken of this. He would tell Carla it was because of her infection. It was entirely plausible. And he would not lose Muriel. He could not lose her, he knew that now.

Weekend drivers changing lanes without signalling. It infuriated him. What would he say to his daughters? And his friends, would any remain? Muriel had wonderful friends but he had always stayed at the periphery. Fifty-seven years old and no friends! He hated Muriel for putting him through this, making him choose. He hated the backup of holiday traffic.

Atrocity bestows its own sainthood. In his monumental suffering, Robin Colby had become a holy man. Nathan had never sought personal advice, but very little humility is required to bare one's soul to the dying.

"You once said that a woman kept at the proper distance offers the consolation that a wife cannot," Nathan said to the benign moonface set now atop a heap of bandaged limbs. "I have to ask you, if such women offer salvation, why you've stayed married to a woman you despise."

"I don't despise Reena. What gave you that idea?"

"All your affairs. The things you said about her. About how you had no sexual feelings for her."

"Oh c'mon, Nathan. You can't compare affairs and marriage!"

"You said affairs are what keep us alive, I think. The woman who retains her sheen? Relief from mortal anxiety, wasn't that it?"

"Yes, yes, Nathan, but it's an illusion. Religion for the churchless, eh?" Robin's laugh was shrill.

"Whatever," Nathan said.

"A mistress is not reality, Nathan. Reena is full of darkness. She confronts me every day with her imperfection, her indefiniteness. It's disempowering. Of course, by comparison a mistress is consoling."

"Consoling only because you keep far enough away to maintain the illusion," Nathan said. "But why stay married if a wife is disempowering, as you put it?"

"Because that's reality, Nathan. I find ambiguities in Reena that I find in myself."

"Why confront death everywhere, Robin? Isn't it enough that we have to deal with our own mortality? Do we need to encounter it in our women as well?"

"Oh, poor Nathan! It's that old riddle. Which is the *true* reality? That's the oldest riddle, isn't it?"

"So this darkness we encounter in a wife, this foreshadowing of our own mortality, are you saying we should embrace it because it's the truth? Is that what you want to tell me, Robin?"

"It depends on whether or not you want to hear it."

"You not only look like a Buddha," Nathan told him, "you sound like one." He was growing impatient, anxious. "Are you saying that's what marriage is? Surrender to death? Who are you kidding, Robin? It's easy for you to talk of surrender now." Nathan knew immediately that he had overstepped and was filled with regret.

Robin's reply was gentle. "You wanted to know why I stayed married. I thought you meant before this happened."

"Yes, of course," Nathan said. "I'm sorry." It was difficult to trust Robin's new magnanimity.

"What I'm saying," Robin continued in a hoarse voice, "is that the shining ideal is not a *real* consolation."

"And so," Nathan took up the thread, "we must cleave to the disempowering woman despite the fact that we countenance our own mortality in her."

"*Because* of that, Nathan. Not in spite of it." Robin was weary. "We cleave to her for companionship," he said.

"Surely, that can't be all!" Nathan was confounded.

"It's the best we can hope for," Robin replied. "Someone to breakfast with, to breathe beside. A companion in the struggle to accept mortality is no small thing."

"It's so pedestrian."

Robin chuckled. "Yes, it's terrifying," he said. "Terrifyingly pedestrian!" He managed a histrionic sigh.

Nathan wanted to throttle his friend. Finally, he pushed on, "Are you happy you stayed married?"

"I never considered any other possibility."

"Didn't you ever fall in love with one of your other women?" Nathan asked.

"Yes, of course," Robin replied. "It was wonderful." His speech was slurred. Nathan could see he was dozing.

"Thank you," he said to the whiteness. Sheets and

gauze. He's falling apart, Nathan thought. Still, the poor bastard gave me something. Nathan wasn't sure what it was that Robin had given him. But he said "thank you" again and left.

At 103rd Street, he parked his car and rang the bell in Muriel's lobby. They would talk, he had decided. He couldn't decide much beyond that. They would work something out.

"No," she said. It would not be convenient for him to come up. "No, later would not be good either."

He slumped back in his chair at the West End Cafe. He would have to avoid the Upper West Side, he thought. Lincoln Center. Carnegie Hall. Eclair. But also the Rockefeller concerts. And Kaufman Concert Hall. And the Brooklyn Academy of Music. He would sense her everywhere. He would become a recluse. He would listen to music at home. But not to Liszt.

He paid the bartender and bid him a moist farewell.

Carla was silent and dense beneath the covers. Safe in her rose-printed gown. Safe on her side of the line that divided their bed. The boundary she observed so carefully. Even in her sleep.

He considered his wife. Someone to breathe beside. It would never be enough. But it was, perhaps, something. Something, perhaps, irreplaceable. He studied the plateau of her hip. She, unlike the others, did not form a cello. He placed his hand on the highest point and moved slowly toward her knee where warm skin extended below the hem of her gown. He reversed the motion and moved up along her flank. Her belly protruded under his fingers. There was, after all, a great comfort in this. She rolled away from him.

"Carla," he said cautiously, "I know it's been awhile."

"No," she said.

"I'm your husband," he said.

"I can't," she said. She did not turn to face him.

"Carla, dear, I think we might reconsider," he said.

119

She sat up and swung her feet over her side of the bed. "I'm importunate, Carla," he said with a small laugh. Finally, she turned to him. "I'm not well," she said. "It's erupting again. I can't."

Dr. Nathan Kline stood on the terrace facing south over Gramercy Park. An old recording spun on his phonograph. *"Mir war auf dieser Welt das Gluck nicht hold!"* *Auch mir*, Nathan thought. Fortune has not been kind to me either. *"Still ist mein Herz und harret seiner Stunde!"* Ah! poor little Gustav Mahler, Nathan thought. You seem so wise and yet, you were so naive. You and I both, little Gustav. We have both been so naive!

Twenty-one.

Hilda, he thought upon reflection, might have shown *some* emotion. Alarm. Sadness. Compassion. But she had been impassive as she gave him the news. The applications to renew his grants had been denied. Both of them. Both projects terminated. The one in its eighteenth year and the more recent project too. It was terminated. No appeal, she had said. Terminated. Heany wanted the labs dismantled by year's end. Two months, she said. She wanted to discuss her severance. That was something he recalled when he began remembering it. She had wanted to discuss her severance. He had had a sharp pain in his left arm. And he'd taken a fistful of Percocets. And some vodka. It was quite a while before he could begin to remember these things.

But once the remembering began there was no forgetting. Each morning at four he woke to remembering. It bore upon him, a crushing weight, some abomination with no boundaries. It distinguished his waking from his sleep. Dull pain in his jaw, his chest. He lay there helpless before his pain, so engrossed was he in his rememberings. And decades would pass. Awful decades of words he regretted saying. Decades of wounds he had inflicted. I am unforgivable, he thought. And all the wounds he had suffered. Others are unforgivable, he thought. It seemed he had always lived in this darkness and that it could not end. I have become my father, after all, he would conclude. When he finally rose to urinate, he was exhausted. He shoved the toothbrush back toward his molars and retched. That was how he began his days. Decades of rememberings, and then the retching.

His days were small and forgotten. Wisps trailing behind the decades of remembering. Even as he peered through his loops, measured the pressure in an eye, offered some cordiality to an old patient, studied Doris Needham's meticulous notations, the rememberings kept up their incessant thrum.

Tom and Armand faced Carla and him on the tennis court in the pear orchard. He snarled at Armand. He barked at Carla. He smiled small smiles at Tom. It was good to keep moving. The dark weight broke a bit when he moved about the court.

"My shoulder's no good," he would announce after a double fault.

"I thought it was the left shoulder," Armand said.

"It was," he replied. "Now it's both shoulders. No feeling in my left hand. Calcium deposits, most likely."

"You ought to get it checked," Tom said.

"Yeah," he said. He was often surprised to hear himself in conversation. To hear his voice through his darkness. To hear others respond as if he had made sense. They were so far away, he could not imagine how they heard him.

He wondered if calcium deposits could really produce that numbness in his left hand. He wondered about the pain in his shoulders. Mostly, he did not think about it.

"I can prescribe Tofranil," Lily told him, "but you really ought to talk to someone, too."

121

"With all due respect to your profession," he said, "I don't think there's anyone I want to talk to. I'll talk to you, if that's okay. And I can prescribe my own Tofranil."

"Of course, we can talk, Nathan, but it's not the same thing. And you're not going to prescribe for yourself." She handed him a prescription.

"You're still awfully pretty," he said. "You're sexy, too, Lily. If I could get it up just now. . ."

"Thanks for the compliment," she said.

"Really, Lily, how come you never remarried?" They were leaving her office now, heading to Le Veau d'Or.

"You've been out with a lot of men, God knows," he continued when they were seated. "Didn't Carla fix you up with Armand? She introduces everyone to Armand. Too bad you didn't like him. He's loaded, you know."

"He wasn't any more or less defective than the others."

"Lily, Lily. You're being much too harsh," he said.

"Have you any idea what the available sampling of men is like?" She was laughing. "You know before you get to dessert why their wives left them."

"There must be some widowers," Nathan offered.

Lily leaned forward and traced a finger round the rim of her wineglass. "Have you ever passed some old piece of upholstered furniture left on the street in a fancy neighborhood? Ever consider that someone, maybe a whole family, had that greasy, ragged mess in their living room until yesterday? Every time I see one of those things, I go home and examine my own furniture. Maybe I'm not noticing the wear and tear as the years pass. People with plenty of money keep this awful stuff in their homes. You don't realize it until they throw it out."

"Widowers?" Nathan couldn't keep from laughing.

Lily drained the wine from her glass. "You think all the really terrific men are married. Then one turns up widowed. He takes you out to dinner and you wonder, 'How did anyone put up with such rude manners, with such boring conversation, with such hypochondria for thirty or forty years?' It's amazing what people live with!"

"You of all people, Lily, how could *you* be surprised?"
"These aren't my patients, Nathan. They're the mild-mannered husbands of the women I envy. The ones whose husbands stayed alive and faithful for years of marriage. And then one of these men is across the table, treating me to his monotonous life and I just want to get home."
"People are pedestrian," he said.
"They're vagrant," she said.
"You're really cheering me up, Lily."
"Not you, Nathan. You're still somebody's husband."

February. March. Sundays. Mondays. They all began at four. Tofranil. Percocet. Vodka. Patients who smiled. Patients who complained. Coffee. Vodka. Just a sip. Passover with the Szabos and Tilly Szabo still not understanding it at all. Sweet wine and another Percocet. His daughters sat silently at the Seder table, staring at their plates.
"Poor Daddy," Alexandra said when they had a moment alone. "You're sadder than I've ever seen you."
"I miss the lab, sweetheart. It's a big step down. And, of course, now I'll never be made chief."
"Do you ever think of getting a divorce?" she asked.
"Alex, how could you ask me that?" He was reeling.
"You and Mom are miserable. And it's getting worse."
"It's not true," he said. "And even if it were, it's none of your business."
"Of course it's my business," she said. "And it's true, Daddy. Anyone can see. A divorce wouldn't be a bad thing, you know."
"It's too late," he said. "I can't live alone like Armand. I don't envy him his women. Not at our age. Besides, who would want me? I'm like a greasy old sofa with its stuffing hanging out. The kind people leave on the sidewalk as trash."
"You'd be more attractive if you were happy," she said.
"Your mother and I have a history. Two terrific daughters." He kissed her tight curls. "We have two homes we've

shared for years and scores of friends who see us as a couple."

"They're mistaken," she said ruefully.

"Don't be angry with me, sweetheart," he said. "We have something. Something more than Armand has. Trust me."

"I love you, Daddy," she said, "but I hate your being so miserable. I don't want you staying married for my sake."

Alexandra would never be the same for him after this. She would remain his friend, but he would approach her cautiously. He had lost his position with her, his place in her eyes. He would never be entirely comfortable with her again.

A woman pressed her back against the slats of an Adirondack chair. They were at the edge of the lake, just a few yards from the Peekskill house. She had silky red hair and skin as white as talc. There was something steamy about her. Not tropical, of course. Not with that complexion. But steamy in the way of indoor swimming pools in roadside motels.

He was aware that his wife had stayed in touch with her college friends, but he hadn't actually seen Grace Nussbaum since that afternoon long ago at the Princeton Club. He remembered her, though. She'd been a very attractive girl.

And now, she looked decent enough although her two divorces came as no surprise. One of those well-meaning women doomed to carry through life an utterly fatal defect in her approach to men. Doomed, too, never to understand her defect. And men could never say just what it was they found so unbearable.

When she'd left for a swim with Carla, Nathan had dozed in his chair. Now, he walked to the little cabana by the lake to change into his trunks.

"I'm terribly sorry," he said, pulling back from the doorway. Grace had tucked a pink towel hastily about her.

"Not at all," she smiled. In one astonishing moment she

pulled him into the aromatic cedar box, shut and locked the door behind him, and let go the towel that had barely contained her.

"Grace," he began.

"Carla told me to." It was the gentle reassuring voice of a school nurse following protocol.

"Carla?"

"She said you've been so depressed lately. She said your girlfriend left you and you lost the grants for your research and that she can't. . ."

"My girlfriend!" He was succumbing to the cedar scent. Grace had stooped to pick up her towel but ended by kneeling on it. She turned her damp white face toward him.

"Carla feels terrible that she can't do for you." She tugged at the zipper on his shorts. "She said you found me attractive."

She was, not surprisingly, very skillful at her work. The horror of what was happening to him added a certain piquancy. She made a display of swallowing hard.

"Thank you," Nathan said. His hands rested on her red hair. He could think of nothing else to say. Then, "I don't think we should leave together. Would you mind going out first?"

"Of course not," Grace said. "I understand completely."

Nathan locked the door behind her and fell back against the cedar panels. He had never in his life been able to weep and he could not do so now. He stared at the sink, unable to regard himself in the mirror. It was as close as he could come to weeping.

PART THREE

Twenty-two.

A star begins as dust. A swirl of particles drawn by gravity, drawn so powerfully the temperature within is driven to numbers requiring logarithmic expression. Hydrogen and helium create and destroy each other. Carbon circles round upon itself. A star is a Mesopotamian bazaar where primordial elements are exchanged one for the other, a frenzied cycle of attractions and repulsions, the oscillations of love gone mad. But it pulsates rhythmically as the chest of a peaceful dreamer. Taken as a whole, viewed from a distance, this is a stable state of affairs. It can continue for billions of years, at a constant temperature, producing an unvarying hue.

But as it comes to the end of its time, a star's internal struggles become more ferocious, more apparent, even from afar. The glowing bits of dust fall upon one another with greater force. It grows dense and small until its particles reignite and burst out again into glowing clouds. Stars continue like this, growing larger and then smaller, each pulsation more exaggerated than its predecessor. Finally, some implode. They are sucked into themselves and become cold dense rocks hurtling through the universe. Others spill, out of control, into bloated swells of cooling specks.

Red dwarfs. White dwarfs. Red giants. A dying star is unbalanced, desperate, deranged. In its death throes, violent or melancholy, it is always grotesque. It is a thing abandoning its own identity. In its ultimate phase, it bears little resemblance to what it has been for uncounted millenia. A dying star is no longer itself.

Nathan could mingle affably, smile politely, and nod as if he were listening. He could peruse *The New York Review of Books* and recite the gist of some recent article to whomever was not-quite-facing him at cocktails. It was important on these occasions to move from one guest to another with alacrity, not to linger. There were scores of dinner parties, some of them their own. He found it difficult to differentiate them. It was his sixtieth year.

Tilly Szabo was carrying a tray laden with those pink-and-white-smeared crackers his wife used to serve. He hated people smearing his crackers for him, making them soggy. Tilly had a big heart but no sense at all when it came to entertaining. Of course, the food would be fine and plentiful. Money, Nathan decided, has certain uneclipsable virtues.

Armand had yet another woman. It was an awkward business for everyone, Armand's women. Faces, names, slender details of lives lived elsewhere. They carried plates to Armand's dining table as if they owned them. They bathed him in endearments filled with anticipation, and then they vanished. Nathan wanted to tell these women that they were doomed, to urge them to flee the darkly handsome man with his melancholic eyes, his art collection, and his Jacuzzi. To flee before they embarrassed themselves. But Carla defended Armand.

"He's terribly lonely," she would tell Nathan as they drove home after dinner at Armand's. "He says he wants to settle down, but he won't just settle."

"Very neat," Nathan would say. "He'll never settle down with any of those we've met. He should have stayed with Zoe."

"He's afraid he'll make another mistake," she'd say.

"He's not taking it seriously," Nathan would say. And then they would be home and undress and go to bed.

The Szabos had invited the usual people. At Carla's instigation, Lily was there to meet Lew Perrin, now a wealthy widower and, Carla said, the best man on the market. Reena Colby arrived late. Her hair was matted, her face vacant. She wishes Robin would die, Nathan thought.

Reena had her son, Marco, in tow. Marco had shot a deer on their front porch. He'd had the venison dressed and roasted for the Szabos. It would be served for dinner but there was also game hen for those who preferred.

And, of course, there was a couple no one had met before. A short, dry man with protruding eyes and a noisy wife. She talked incessantly of his hobby. His sculpture filled his office, crowded their home. "He's a born sculptor," she said.

"What kind of sculpture?" Nathan asked politely.

"People, of course," the man replied. "Only people. The human form is all that interests me. Children. Men. Women. In every imaginable activity. I want to render every human activity in clay."

"Then you build up, you don't chip away. No marble or wood," Nathan said.

"No chipping away," the man said. He was a surgeon. Larry Rosbacher. He introduced Nathan to his wife, Elaine.

"Larry loves to work with his hands," Elaine said.

At the table, Tilly placed Larry next to Carla so they could talk about sculpture. Nathan sat opposite. Armand's date was at Larry's right.

"And which is *your* husband?" Larry asked the woman.

"No one," she said. "I'm Vera." She had a rich, easy smile and her gleaming dark hair was swept back from her face, woven into a thick braid that lay heavy on her back. "I'm here with him," she said, indicating Armand at the far end of the table.

"I came with her," Rosbacher said, nudging his chin toward his wife. "We're a pair."

"So you always come together," Vera said, her smile broadening as she skewered a bit of venison. Larry hesitated, unsure about her joke.

"When you speak of sculpting, you sound like the Lord on the sixth day," she continued. She was toying with him. Nathan saw deep intelligence in her, and irony and mischief as well. Her grey eyes twinkled.

"I am, in fact, very much like God," Rosbacher replied.

"But far more modest," Vera said. The buzz of conversation around the table had subsided.

"I mean my work," Rosbacher said. "In my work, I'm *required* to be God. Each day I make profound, excruciating decisions." He said this with compelling gravity.

"What decisions?" Vera asked. "What exactly do you do?"

"I'm a neonatal urologist," he said.

"I thought urologists had *elderly* patients," Vera said. "What do you do with newborns?"

"My patients are born with indeterminate sex organs or none at all," Rosbacher said. Now the attention of the group was riveted on him. He had used the woman for this moment, Nathan thought, had made her his unwitting shill.

"They're hermaphrodites," Rosbacher continued. "I have forty-eight hours to decide their sexes and give them definitive organs. So, you see, I am always a sculptor, always creating people."

There was a murmur at the table. He's given this speech before, Nathan decided. In just this way. Waits for silence and then . . . his denoument.

"Aren't there genetic indications? Natural codings, so to speak? You don't make these decisions in a vacuum, do you?" Vera was impressed but also horrified.

"In true hermaphrodites there is no clear genetic information. No clear structural indication. Everywhere you look, you find equivocal signals. That's what's so fascinating."

It's revolting, Nathan thought. He found he could not swallow a half-chewed morsel of venison; he spit it into his dinner napkin.

"Do you consult with the parents?" Vera asked.

"Not to ascertain their preferences, if that's what you mean. They have no better rights than other parents." Rosbacher was emphatic. He was a man whose business required unwavering principles and policies without exceptions.

"How do you finally decide?" Vera wanted to know.

"Sometimes it's pure intuition. I sculpt all night and in the morning I go to the O.R. and I make a boy or a girl, as it comes to me."

"They must require years of counseling," she said.

"I am opposed to psychotherapy," Rosbacher said. "What I do leaves no emotional scars."

"But in puberty," Vera was agitated, "are the hormones

there? Do they develop proper secondary characteristics?"

"My boys and girls become perfectly normal men and women," Larry Rosbacher said with a reassuring nod.

"I can see why you feel like God," Vera said quietly. She was not admiring, only subdued.

"And you, my dear," Rosbacher said. "Do *you* work at something?" He leaned closer to her, lifting his brows to display the full effect of his bulging eyeballs.

"At something," she replied. She had recovered her ironic demeanor and was regarding him aggressively.

"And what sort of something is that?"

She looked away from Larry and moved her eyes slowly around the table, letting them come to rest on Armand. She stared, unblinking, into his face.

"Well, dear, we're all waiting to hear," Rosbacher cooed.

"And I," Vera said, "am waiting for you to take your hand off my knee." The ironic gaze remained levelled at Armand.

Larry Rosbacher turned crimson but it hardly mattered. A flood of hilarity had broken over the table.

Nathan patted Armand's shoulder as they said good-night.

"She's marvelous," Nathan told him.

"Marvelous," Carla echoed. "Good for you, Armand."

Twenty-three.

Robin Colby's death was a technicality. Authorized persons made notations in ink and the bandages and bones were re-classified.

Nathan paced about the old couch where his father-in-law sat in the cavernous study. The old man's brow was smooth and tan: a speckled egg. The backs of his hands were speckled, too, and crossed by mountains of teal veins. His fingers were buried in thick black fur. Walter, a new cat.

Lisle, now a Semiotics major, was the only one who truly understood her grandfather's theories about correspondences between the shapes of words and the shapes of things. But she was confused about the cats and thought she should be consulted about naming this new one.

"I don't see it as a Walter," she said.

"You will have to take it on faith, then," Felix said. "This cat is Walter. *Bruno* Walter, in fact."

"You've changed the rules for naming them," Lisle protested.

"You are astute as usual," her grandfather beamed. "I think maybe your sister will help you figure it out."

Nathan had figured it out. Felix's mind flashed and crackled, fierce as ever, Nathan thought. Testimony to the triumph of spirit over matter.

"What can I say to eulogize Robin Colby?" he asked the old man. "He was a pig. Everyone knew that. I knew another side of him, but I can't talk about it at his funeral. What a terrible task I've taken on. I don't know why I offered."

"You always offer," Felix said, smiling down at the sleek black coil in his lap.

"That's true," Nathan said. "It's an odd thing I do, eulogizing everyone."

"Not so odd," Felix said without lifting his eyes from Walter. "It separates you from the others, removes you from the death. Empowering is what it is."

"A mistress is empowering," Nathan murmured wistfully.

"What's that?" The old man heard less and less.

"Nothing," Nathan said. "I'll speak about his research, his children. About Reena. This is a terrible eulogy, somehow. Far more difficult than the others."

"Well, of course," Felix said.

"What does that mean, 'of course?'"

"You jousted with him all these years. He was your most

formidable competitor. Now, he's vanquished. You have your wish."

"Go to hell, Felix," Nathan told him. "And take psycho-analysis with you!"

Felix remained in the study, stroking Bruno Walter. He was thinking about his daughter. About the match she'd made. A match *I* made, he thought. I wanted the best for her, he told himself. He considered that, in spite of several earnest attacks upon them, stacks of magazines still remained in the cellar. She was blither, firmer in her step, that was clear. Yet, Felix thought, she has never come to full flower. Her sculpture could be so much more powerful. Her voice, her gestures, could be so much more . . .

He found her in the garden, pulling weeds from the ivy.

Carla stood up and placed her hands on his shoulders. "Papa, it's getting much too cold. You should be in the house now. Come, I'll make you some coffee."

Felix rested his hands on hers. "I've been thinking, *liebchen,* I must apologize."

"Apologize?" Carla had considered for some months that her father's mind tended to wander. She had not yet discussed this with Sophie.

"You were so little, so beautiful. A tiny flower. I held you close to me to keep you safe. We might have lost you in Europe. We might have lost everything. I had to hold you very close to keep you safe."

"I know, Papa. It was a terrible time. I'm very grateful." She leaned her face to his and kissed him lightly.

But Felix drew back. "But, you know, I hurt you, I think. I held you too tight, I never let you breathe your own air. You never learned to. . . ."

"Papa! You've been wonderful. You and Mother both!" It seemed to Carla that her father's self-reproach was the sort of thing men drown in as they begin to die.

"I only want to tell you," Felix continued, "that we have been here in America a very long time now."

"Yes," she said cautiously, "a very long time."

"And we have been safe for a very long time," Felix

continued. "You're no longer the little flower pressed tight in my hand. You are a good strong tree. You don't have to be afraid anymore."

He drew her into an embrace so strong it surprised her. He held her until her breathing became slow and even against his chest. "I'm sorry," he said, "I brought you into a frightening world. But now you can stop being afraid."

Carla began to weep. She did not know what to make of this speech. But her tears gave way to deep, throaty sobs and she let her father hold her until they passed.

A woman with soft grey eyes approached Nathan after Robin Colby's memorial service.

"That was such a moving speech," she said. "He must have been a very good friend."

"Possibly," Nathan replied. "Have we met?"

"Vera Lenz," she said. "At the Szabos. The urologist? God, I think he was."

"Ah, yes," Nathan said. "Of course. Good to see you again." He hadn't thought to remember her. Armand's women went by so rapidly. "What did you say your name was?"

"Vera. Vera Lenz. I'm Armand's. . . ."

"Yes, yes. Lucky man, Armand."

They chatted over wine and cake. There was a brightly-colored Guatemalan shawl draped about her black wool dress, and the dark gypsy hair, again plaited into a thick, impudent rope, hung down her back. She cast a bright beam through the sombre little parlor.

Mourners interrupted with thanks for the eulogy. More wine, more conversation. Her face, Nathan noticed, was remarkably mobile, her eyebrows pulling up high, furrowing her brow when the grey eyes widened. Her hands darted constantly, punctuating her thoughts, hands that tapered into surprisingly long fingers. Nathan struggled to match the husky voice to this small, wiry woman. This woman, he decided as they spoke, is astonishing in her warmth, penetrating in her perceptions. Nathan had the sensation of mandolins, of dancers circling.

Armand came for her. "We're leaving, sweetie. Nathan and Carla are coming over later for supper. See you tonight, Nathan."

She had potted a chicken and made dumplings. Armand had set the table with French country faience.

"My mother never made it this well," Nathan said as he ladled more yellow liquid into his bowl. "Carla doesn't cook like this. In fact, no one we know cooks like this. It's quite original of you, Vera, to be so old-fashioned."

There were brandies with the coffee and warm apple and nut pie. Vivaldi. And laughter. Vera made the brooding Armand laugh, Nathan noticed. He followed her into the kitchen.

"So who *are* you, actually?" he began. "I mean, where are you from? How do you know Armand?" He'd had too much brandy. Her answers passed through him. Her gaze, it seemed, made him shrink back and squint. The confusion of waking into sunlight.

"Do you have children? Do you work somewhere?" These were questions he was accustomed to asking and they anchored him.

She had two children. She taught.

"Yes?"

"At Columbia. Teachers' College. I teach art therapy."

"*I'm* a Columbia man, you know. An ophthalmologist. I'm at N.Y.U. now. Until recently, I directed research there. Cancer research."

"That's wonderful," she beamed. "I'm doing research now. On a grant."

Nathan leaned back against the kitchen counter. A heaviness pressed upon him, compacting him. He was uncertain of his size, his height, his volume.

"That's very, very nice," he finally managed to say.

"It's stressful," she said, "but also stimulating." She was scraping plates, stacking them in the dishwasher, scouring pots as she spoke. It was disorienting. He really did hate kitchens. "Autistic children," she said. "We're studying their paintings."

137

"Remarkable," he said. "Are you the principal investigator?"

"Oh no," she said, "just assisting. I also teach two days at the college and also one morning a week with preschoolers at the synagogue. Then I have my own two boys. I'm pretty busy," she smiled.

Nathan's eyes followed her about the kitchen. "I loved *my* projects," he said. "They were my life." His lips, his jaw had turned to stone. "They're gone now."

Vera's gaze had become an immense embrace; he thought he might dissolve in it. Unbearable. He put his hand to his face, then pulled it away and stared at it, aghast. It was wet with tears. "My God!" he said.

"It's all right," she said softly. "Tears are cleansing."

"I never cry," Nathan began.

"Sweetie, come join us by the fire," he heard Armand call to her.

"It's all right," Vera reassured him.

"Go ahead," he said. "I'm okay. Just a little drunk."

They were sitting by the hearth. Carla on the great brocade armchair, the glow of embers reflected on her cheek. Vera lolling on the floor, her head in Armand's lap. She rose when Nathan entered and drew up a chair for him.

The Four Seasons, Nathan thought. Vivaldi and a glowing fire. It really is too much. Armand might have a taste for paintings, but he's utterly naive about music.

"Do you enjoy music?" he asked Vera. She was standing now, behind Armand's chair, her fingers rubbing his hair, his temples. She slid her hands along his neck to his shoulders and dug her thumbs into his back. Armand moaned. Nathan averted his eyes.

"Yes," she said. "I love music."

"Vivaldi?" Nathan asked.

"It *is* a bit of a Christmas card, isn't it?" she smiled. "I mean with the embers and the brandy and all."

"Do *you* like Vivaldi," he asked Armand.

"Uhmmmm," Armand said. His moans deepened as Vera continued, rotating her fingers into his neck, swaying gently behind his chair.

138

"Never mind," Nathan murmured.

Armand's eyes were closed and he flexed his shoulders under Vera's hands. Nathan tucked his chin down as if he were attending to the music. But he heard only Armand. A leonine rumble. A purr. A vast, blissful yawn. He doesn't deserve her, Nathan thought. He knows nothing about music.

He hazarded a second glance at Vera. Her eyes were closed lightly now and she leaned into Armand and then back with the rhythm of her kneading fingers, the swivel of her pelvis barely perceptible. My God, Nathan thought as he felt the erection swell in his trousers. He wished he'd kept his jacket on.

"We should be leaving," he said dryly.

"I love a massage," Armand said. He rubbed his eyes and reached back for Vera's hands to still them. "Let's say good night to our guests, sweetie."

"Terrific dinner," Nathan told Vera at the door.

"Thank you," Vera said. "Glad you enjoyed it." She stretched her slender arms and yawned sweetly.

A jungle creature, Nathan decided. Research. Chicken soup. Velvet eyes. So confusing. He thought he must be very tired.

"And that was a memorable eulogy," Vera was telling him. The eulogy for Robin, it seemed, had occurred ages ago. It had been a terribly long and complicated day.

"Such warmth in that woman," Carla said as she turned into the driveway of the sprawling old house. "I hope Armand appreciates her."

"He doesn't," Nathan said.

He was too tired to read himself to sleep. Too tired to wait for Carla to finish in the bathroom. He pulled the quilt around himself.

A massive figure loomed in the corner, an armored knight. A lance extended, hung with black pennons. Colby! It had to be! Those were Colby's weasel eyes peering through the vizor. And under the armor, Nathan knew, was a man whose skin had flaked away.

"Jesus Christ!" he exhaled. He rolled over, pulled the quilt higher over his head and hugged himself.

Carla's hand was on his arm as he sat up with a convulsive jerk.

"You were having a nightmare," she said. "I couldn't wake you. Are you okay? Oh, Nathan! You're sweating!"

"I'm sorry," he said.

"Can I get you something? Some water?"

"No, Carla, I'm okay. I'm sorry I woke you." He turned his pillow and lay back on it. "Did I cry out?"

"Several times," she said. "Something about a massage. You seemed to be protesting."

"Robin," he said.

"Robin?"

"Robin. He was rubbing my neck and my back. Rubbing his hands all over my skin. It started out as Armand, but then it was Robin. And I was melting, dissolving. My skin was coming off."

"Dreams are so strange," she said.

"I'm sorry I disturbed you, Carla. Go back to sleep."

The air in the bedroom was clotted and his bedlinens sodden with sweat. His daughters, his in-laws, were asleep. The huge study rattled. The kitchen was unendurable, the living room icy.

There simply was no place to pass the night.

Twenty-four.

Somehow, it was September again. His daughters would soon depart for school. Felix and Sophie would head south; they no longer waited for the autumn chill to toll. He would be left with Carla and the thickness that lay between them.

"Just be sure to bring Vera," he heard his wife say into the telephone. "Nathan is more irritable than ever. He's upset that I'm giving a party in honor of Nina's book. Vera has a really cheering effect on him. Be sure she comes along."

He backed quickly out of the room but it was clear that he had overheard.

"Armand's having problems with Vera," Carla said. "I persuaded him to bring her to the party. You ought to talk with him. Tell him how much we like her."

Nina Phillips's autobiography, he thought, must be a hideous book. He was certain he would never read it. Worse than the book itself was the prospect of this party. Nina Phillips in *his* home, sitting on *his* chairs. Castrated, mutilated. Crossing her panty-hosed legs, brushing her hair back from her electrolysized face.

Carla had invited everyone they knew and some they had never met. Phil's college roomate, for example. Mike Ross.

"How is *he* going to feel?" Nathan demanded to know.

"Only you have a problem with it," she said. "I need to do this, Nathan. I've spent so many years not understanding. Now everything is finally all right."

She wore a pale blue cashmere sweater he hadn't seen in years and a gold bracelet he could not recall. Tiny baubles dangled from it: a tennis racquet, a sailboat, a heart, a Yale key.

By the window overlooking the lake, surrounded by Tom, Stew Abrams, and Mike Ross, stood Vera, dark pendulum of a braid against her narrow back, her body animated as she spoke.

"Men always flock to you, don't they?" Nathan said, planting a kiss on her cheek.

"Your guest of honor is a lovely woman," Vera said, nodding in Nina's direction.

"She gives me the creeps," Nathan said.

Armand rushed toward them. "Jesus, Nathan! I sat down right next to him. To *her*. She *looks* like a woman. God, it made me queasy."

141

"Perhaps we should step out onto the porch," Nathan suggested.

"You're both overreacting," Vera said. "Nina Phillips is a really sweet woman."

"Give Nina our regards," Nathan said, ushering Armand to the porch.

"Vera's the best woman you've ever known," Nathan told Armand when they were alone. "You're not thinking of giving her up, I hope."

"She's like the others," Armand sighed. "Marriage. It's all they think about."

"She's not at all like the others," Nathan insisted. "We've met the others. Vera is an absolute original. And she's funny, she makes you laugh. Haven't you realized how much she cheers you?" He took Armand's elbow and led him away from the house and down the sloping lawn toward the lake. "We've all noticed the difference she's made. She's so vital, so alive." Nathan's voice dropped and he slowed his pace. "It's clear she loves you," he told Armand. "The love of a good woman is a powerful thing, you know."

"Maybe too powerful for me just now," Armand mused.

They turned and started walking back to the house.

"I'll tell you this much," Nathan said. "If you don't marry her. . ."

"Yes," Armand said, "if I don't marry her, I should have my head examined."

"What I was going to say," Nathan continued, a boyish grin lighting his face, "was if you don't marry her. . .uh, _I_ will!"

"That's quite a challenge," Armand laughed.

They were still laughing as they returned to the party. Nina stood tall beside the piano, her willowy arms slung about the shoulders of Carla and Mike Ross. Sifting through old photos.

"How could she have done this?" Armand wondered aloud.

"You mean Nina?"

"Well, Nina too. But I meant Carla. This really is a terrible party."

"Please," Nathan said, "you don't know the half of it. She's wearing Phil Neuman's class key. For friendship's sake."

"Good God!" Armand said.

Over the grey linoleum his patients came and went, following the tiny squeaks of Doris Needham's crepe-soled shoes.

"Good Yom Tov!" said one elderly man.

"A happy New Year!" said another.

"Happy New Year to you," Nathan replied.

The holidays always surprised him. He hadn't attended holiday services since he'd left for college. His wife had left Judaism behind in the *mitteleurope* that had almost cost her life. Alex had become quite religious and had often rebuked them both for their laxity. Today, his patients' good wishes embarrassed him.

"Will you be finishing early this evening?" Doris Needham wanted to know. "I mean, with your holiday and all."

His holiday? Well, it *was* his holiday. A sharp twinge dissolved in nostalgia. *Tekiah! Teruah!* He remembered the words that called forth the blasts of the *shofar!* He remembered its plaintive wail. And his father's hand extending from the hem of a *tallis* and resting on his shoulder. Some years, it would be his birthday and Rosh Hashonah on the same day.

"Yes," he said. "It's a very important holiday, Mrs. Needham. Ring Alex for me, would you please?"

Alexandra was overjoyed. She would meet him at the little synagogue on Gramercy Park. They might have to stand in the rear but it would be worth it.

"*Tekiah! Teruah!*" he sang out as he embraced her. She wrapped her arms about his neck. She was beginning to be pretty, he thought. She deserves a boyfriend, this daughter of mine.

143

A cellist accompanied the cantor. What gorgeous music, Nathan thought. He thumbed through the *Siddur*, racing ahead to the text for the next day. It was there, just where he remembered it. After the *Kaddish,* a "Meditation":

> "And remember that the companionship of Time
> is but of short duration. It flies more quickly
> than the shades of evening. We are like a child
> that grasps in his hand a sunbeam. He opens his
> hand soon again but, to his amazement, finds it
> empty and the brightness gone."

What is this, he wondered. How did it come to be in the *Rosh Hashonah* liturgy? Not a prayer, not a portion of the Torah. There were others, he realized, peppering the service. They're never read aloud, these little poems. Who put them here? He withdrew a pen and a bit of paper from his breast pocket and quickly noted the words.

The companionship of Time. Odd, he reflected. He had always considered Time an enemy.

"This was grand," he told Alexandra as they walked home around the Park. "Thank you for accompanying me."

"We'll go back tomorrow," she said.

Lisle thrust herself against him as he let himself through the apartment door. Felix. An afternoon nap from which he never woke.

He held his rosy daughter close and nuzzled her fragrant hair. He could not recall the womanly shape of her. Perhaps he had never known it. He remembered only a radiant, succulent child. She had, it seemed, worn garlands. And then she had become lost to him. She was her grandfather's favorite. He had given her the name she was called. Since her earliest days, they had shared some secret and mysterious bond. Poor Lisle, he thought. And Alex, too. Their first death. He wanted to wrap them both in their nursery quilts and trundle them off in a wooden shoe.

"You'll have another eulogy, Daddy," Alex said.

"I'm afraid my eulogizing days are over."

"But you'll have to," Alex said. "Who else can do it?"

Nathan thought of the day he had stood in Butler Library, conjuring an image of Felix Weisenthal. Of Felix cheering him on as he. . . That really was so long ago.

Nathan vowed to his wife and his daughters that his eulogy for Felix would be his last.

"You're a wonderful son-in-law," Sophie told him. "Felix would have been so pleased."

"I'm not so sure," Nathan said. "He told me it's my way of escaping death, my way of conquering it."

"That's silly," Sophie said.

"Perhaps he was right," Nathan told her. "Perhaps it's a little game I play with myself."

But he knew the game was over. Felix had ruined eulogies and left him with a huge, cold battleship hauled up close against his cheek. He wondered how Lew, how Lily, even Hassah with that splendid old cat, had ever endured it: being so close to it, holding it in their hands. The inutterable fact of terminus.

"My father-in-law was a doctor who did not imagine himself a scientist," he told the throng at Riverside Chapel. "He did not view the human soul as a proper subject for scientific inquiry. He told me, when my first child was born, that I was foolish not to realize what to him was obvious: that no amount of empirically verifiable speculation, however sophisticated, could ever account for the processes of the human soul. I dismissed this as old-fashioned poppycock. I still don't know if it is anything more.

"I do know, however, that Felix Weisenthal's view is the logical requirement of a belief that something of the human spirit survives those processes which we know with scientific certainty occur in death. In the case of Felix's spirit, I certainly hope he was right."

He discoursed for awhile on Felix's accomplishments, his publications and contributions to psychoanalytic theory. Then he read the little meditation he had copied from the *Siddur* two days earlier.

145

". . .We are like a child that grasps in his hand a sunbeam. He opens his hand soon again but, to his amazement, finds it empty and the brightness gone.

"Felix Weisenthal thoroughly enjoyed the companionship of Time," he told the mourners. "He was a sunbeam that we were each honored to grasp for some short time. I do not believe his brightness will soon be gone."

"Thank you, Nathan," Carla said. "It was your best eulogy ever."

"Great speech," Armand told him. "You're really good at this sort of thing."

"It was my last one," Nathan said. His fingertips and the inside of his mouth felt icy. "Where's Vera?" he asked Armand.

"It's over," Armand said very softly. Nathan thought his friend was about to cry.

"I'm awfully sorry to hear that," he said. "Now the brightness really *is* gone."

Twenty-five.

"Grey," the nurse had said. She said he looked grey, that he should lie down for awhile. He'd said it was just a touch of vertigo. The events of the last three days, he'd said, had worn him out. A death in the family, the girls leaving for school, his wife going south to settle her mother. He hadn't been eating. "And the holidays," he said. "You know how it gets during the holidays."

He'd wanted to resume the stress test immediately. He felt okay, he'd said. He would finish the treadmill in no time at all. He needed to renew his pilot's license before it expired. He'd forgotten the deadline, what with the holidays. She'd said he still looked grey. "Stay on your back and breathe slowly," she'd said. As though he weren't a doctor. As though she didn't know who he was.

"And the heat was a factor," he'd explained. "Indian

summer and *Rosh Hashonah* always come together."

She'd begun sticking the little rubber cups to his chest with petroleum jelly. "This is silly," he'd said. "I know you want to be especially careful. I *am* on the faculty, of course. But this is really too much."

The needle began its scratchings. The glossy paper unspooled. He had heard it.

"You really don't need to draw blood," he'd told her. "A bit of vertigo, that's all."

"The cardiologist's orders," she'd said.

"I don't have a cardiologist," he'd insisted. "And I really must get on with the stress test."

"We're going to have to finish that another time," she'd said sweetly.

"Do you know who I am?"

"Yes, Dr. Kline, I do. Dr. Taylor will be in to see you shortly."

How many times, he wondered, had he operated on an eye, cut through a man's eye? They would shudder in horror as he told them they needed surgery. "I cannot let you do that," they would say. They would plead for alternatives. "Better you should take the knife to my testicles," they would say. "It would be easier if you operated on my heart," they would say. "A knife in the eye! I cannot think of such a thing!"

He would tell them they would feel nothing. They would be asleep.

"I cannot sleep," they would say. "How can I sleep imagining a knife in my eye?"

He would be seamless reassurance, seamless optimism. He'd taken years acquiring such impassiveness.

And now, Dr. Taylor was telling him, him, Nathan Kline, that they would cut into his heart with a knife. His heart. They would open his chest and set his heart in ice. A finely trained team of surgeons. They would cut into it with a knife. Taylor's seamlessness left no doubt. It would be done.

He found his way home. The apartment, its furnishings, were retracted and noncommittal. He poured a Stolichnaya and sat at the harpsichord, gazing out across Gramercy Park.

He had never really understood their fears. "Better my testicles than my eyes," they had said. Phil Neuman gave up his testicles and more. "My God," he wondered aloud, "however did he do that?" He, himself, cut into eyes every week. It can't be easier to give up a testicle, he thought.

And a heart, what of a heart? Better a testicle than an eye. Better an eye than a heart. Where, he wondered, where does a man really live?

There would be weeks to endure. Tests. Measurements. It wasn't an emergency, Taylor had said. He would have a second opinion. He would go to New Jersey where his father's cardiologist still practiced. If they were going to open his chest and take out his heart, it would be close to where he'd been born. People would be upset, he knew. It would be difficult to visit him in a hospital in New Jersey. Carla will say I'm being difficult. I'm always being difficult. Too bad, he thought, I can be difficult if they're taking out my heart. Cutting it up with a knife. *That's* difficult.

Across Gramercy Park, people spilled from the little synagogue like dark ink. Kol Nidre, he realized. The eve of the Day of Atonement. Of Yom Kippur. They had begun their fast and said their prayers and were returning home to sleep.

On Rosh Hashonah our fate is written. Who shall live and who shall die. On Yom Kippur, our fate is sealed. He could not imagine how he remembered these fragments of liturgy. Ancient fragments, buried in some melodic ritual. Buried in the chants of swaying, white-robed priests. In New Jersey, beside his father. These fragments had slipped into his memory then and stayed there, buried until now. He would go to New Jersey, to his father's man.

On Yom Kippur our fates are sealed. Who shall live and who shall die. He would go too, he knew, to the service at the little synagogue tomorrow. Three times during the morning he would read aloud an extensive list of transgressions and, as he called out the name of each one in turn, he would beat his fist against his chest. For the sin of being stiff-necked. Beat. For the sin of coveting. Beat. He would go alone and beat his chest.

He stepped out onto the terrace. It had grown cool. He wanted to tell someone. Not his daughters. Not his wife. A friend is what was wanted. I might have told Colby, he thought. Or Felix. Doctors who would understand. As it was, it seemed there was no one.

"What is man?" he read in a little rhyme inserted between the prayers. "Man is frail. . .like an aimless child. . .who stumbling, falls and resumes his struggle. . .seeking more and more of wealth and power. . .Til at last death comes to overtake him."

"*Piyyut*," it was called. There were many *Piyyutim,* some quite elaborate. Whose thoughts are these, he wondered once again.

> "But of man—ah! the tale is another
> His counsels are evil and vain
> He dwells with deceit as a brother
> And the worm is the close of his reign.
> Into earth he is carted and shovelled
> And who shall recount or who heeds
> When above earth he strutted or grovelled
> His marvellous deeds?
> NOT SO GOD! Earth on nothing He founded
> And on emptiness stretched out the sky. . . .

I'm sufficiently humbled, Nathan concluded, and he shut the *Siddur* and left the synagogue.

The tests went on for weeks. Weeks of hospital forms, of syringes and questionnaires. Was he allergic to anything? Weeks of telephone calls. To his daughters. They must not worry and surely not return home. To his lawyers to review his will. To his insurance broker. To Heaney, and Mrs. Needham. "Three weeks," he told her. "Tell my patients I'll be away for three weeks."

He called Armand and then he could not recall why. "Would you like to have dinner?" Armand asked him. He was terribly lonely, Nathan knew. They dined at the Oyster Bar where, as usual, the smelts were excellent and the white tile floor was surgically scrubbed. Weeks passed. It was already November.

There is a shade of lavender rent with orange that is November dusk. A lavender sky stretched out unnoticed behind towers at the rim of Central Park. Surrounding the towers, plastering them, with numinousness. A demure young woman whose cheeks were frosted apples, whose eyes were watery with cold, pressed forward to meet him, her hands buried in a fur muff. A fur muff that suited her so perfectly, Nathan could have leapt to embrace her. But he kept his reserve and chatted about the chill in the air and took no note of that particular shade of lavender, blue enough to herald December, rosy enough to console the brown leaves.

Impersonal conversation. He supposed she was coy. She supposed she was seeing him for her father's sake, this exceptional young man. This importunate young man. The lavender sky was, then, what the violinist was, leaning ferociously into his instrument to shield his fingers from the chill air and sending his music out to get lost in it. It was like the pungent musk of burnt chestnuts. It was the air through which they moved, their backdrop, their ambience. Nothing more.

And now, it was everything.

Blue. Rose. They held so much import he could scarcely keep track of his thoughts. He sat on a petrified bench by the Park's boathouse and watched the dusk press down upon those screeching vermillion ribbons. He watched the struggle as the gleaming bands of excitement yielded slowly at first and then capitulated. He gripped the slats of his seat. There was a hole in his glove and the tip of his right index finger was numb. I will yield with exceeding slowness, he decided. I will gleam and screech a shameless orange before it all shuts down.

He got up and crammed his hand into his pocket. It was becoming dark and he felt very cold.

The apartment, too, was very dark and very cold. His wife was once again in Florida tending to her mother, resolving things. Papers and insurance. There was no end to these matters. He was hungry and chilled. He cleared his throat as he dialed.

"Vera," he said. "It's Nathan Kline. This is Nathan, Vera. How are you? We've missed you."

"Vera," he began again when she had answered his other questions, "I know it's quite late but I wondered . . . I mean if you're free, of course . . .I wondered if you would have dinner with me tonight. I really would like to talk with you."

Twenty-six.

A low, tin ceiling caused the clink and clatter of the crowd to reverberate. Like bells in a small town of churches, pealing all at once. He never could remember that restaurant although he did try to many times thereafter.

He did not remember either—except that she once or twice reminded him—that he had driven her from the restaurant to the Plaza Hotel where, he suggested, they might dance the night away. She was not suitably attired, she had told him. Whereupon he turned east and then south to the Waldorf-Astoria where, he suggested, the Empire Room had a wonderful dance floor. She had wondered if he was drunk. He had said "No," and continued south to the World Trade Center where they'd ordered brandies over New York Harbor.

She was, she later confided, confused and a little alarmed by this behavior. But then, when he told her why he had needed to see her, she had understood.

"When is it going to happen?" she asked. She rested her chin in her left palm. Her fingers climbed her face like vines. She had extraordinary fingers, he decided.

151

"In a few weeks. Early in the new year, I imagine."

"It must be awful having to wait like this."

Nathan's mouth opened wide but the laugh he emitted was a narrow one. "I'm not worried," he told her. "I've known the surgeon for years. Top man."

"How could you not be worried?"

"I know what's involved," he said. "Fear is pointless."

"But real," she insisted. The soft grey eyes, the husky voice. Nathan had often found he had to listen for awhile to get used to it coming from her.

"Why are you dwelling on this?" He ordered another Remy Martin. A double.

"I'm just trying to understand why you wanted to see me. Why you called me tonight." Her voice was low, complicitous.

"I called you because I wanted to talk with you. To see you before . . ."

"Yes?"

"Because I've *always* wanted to see you. To invite you to dinner. But there was Armand."

"And Carla," she said. "Where is Carla, anyway?"

"Down in Florida with her mother. Felix died, you know."

"I didn't know. How terrible. This really is a nasty time for you."

"Actually, it's a wonderful time," he said. "An absolutely splendid time. Because I am here at the top of the City talking with you and your fingers are the longest, most graceful fingers I think I have ever seen. And I want you to come dancing with me. I haven't danced in years. I'm an excellent dancer, you know. Disciplined. Smooth. You're a good dancer, too. I can tell."

It was four in the morning and he drove her home. She said she would go dancing with him. Before the surgery. "I promise," she said.

And she did.

He wore the Dusseldorf tuxedo because he found it in his closet among Carla's college blazers and it still fit.

"Carla refused to be seen with me in this," he told Vera. "She gave up the Harvest Ball rather than let me wear it."

"It's very you," she told him. The deep, rich laughter engulfed him.

"I know it's very scary," she said quietly as he fox-trotted her about a crowded floor. "It's scary but you're going to come out just fine. I know you will."

"I need a friend," he said.

"I'm your friend," she said. "I'll keep right on being your friend."

"It's nice having my hand around your waist," he said, "but do I place it under or over the pigtail?"

There was a spaciousness now, and a path through his days. Each chore was but some small diversion from the time he spent with her.

He showed her the architect's plans for renovating his office.

"A perfect new start," she said. "The timing is just right."

He visited her at the preschool and watched her flock swarm about her, grasping at the sparks that cascaded like petals of chrysanthemum fireworks, spilling from her as she skipped from one eager face to the next. The powerful energy of her own face, eyes dancing beneath the raised brows, every feature in motion. Captivating the little ones, entrancing them. The deep voice, its gentle humor. The agile, animated hands. Hands of a magician, Nathan decided.

He met her two fierce sons. Do not harm her, they seemed to say with their cool reserve. She is a treasure and she is ours, they were telling him.

She showed him the drawings the autistic children made. "They really are poets," she said.

They talked about Armand. He asked about her divorce. She asked why he had remained married.

"So you noticed," he said, looking down at his hands.

Vera nodded.

"We have children," he said.

"So do I," she said. "Your daughters would endure a divorce."

"Alex actually urged me to do it."

"That's sad."

"Our finances are complicated, you know. And socially, well, you really do have to be a couple."

"That's absolutely medieval," she said. "In some respects, I think, it's better to be single."

"Armand is single," Nathan said. "He's very unhappy."

"But Armand has the possibility of finding someone he loves. You don't have that possibility."

They spoke of politics. And of art. Of the art of politics and the politics of art.

"Your views are so original," he said. "Like so much else about you. Utterly refreshing. What do you read?"

She laughed that laugh he had come to think of as the sound of her and hunched her shoulders up quizzically as she so often did when she laughed. "I read my children's homework assignments," she said. "No time for much else. Mostly, I just think about things. I'm always thinking about things."

Christmas. He took her to Saks for leather gloves that ran to her elbows. To a tuba concert at Rockefeller Center. To the Russian Tea Room with its incandescent samovars.

One Saturday morning he fetched her and drove to Washington. Matisse's paintings from the Midi. "I want to see these with you," he told her, "because you are an odalisque."

"I'm an art therapist," she said.

"I watched you massage Armand's neck and his back and I realized then that you were an odalisque."

She stood staring at *Pineapples and Anemones* painted in 1939. He moved about the gallery and returned to her.

"Is this really such an interesting painting?" he asked.

"The anemones," she said. "He could never have guessed when he painted them that ten years later he would be bedridden and unable to paint. That he would be forced to begin his cutouts. That these anemones would return years later as his signature in the cutouts. He could not have had the slightest inkling when he made this painting."

Nathan turned to the painting and then back to Vera. She was studying it with sadness, almost pity.

"It's disturbing to see this painting," she went on earnestly, "knowing how those anemones will return and knowing that, at the time he painted them, the painter could not have known."

"Vera," he said, "you *do* think an awful lot."

They drove back to New York very late and, once more, looked out over the Harbor. He told her stories he had not told in years. He remembered things he had not remembered. He talked about a summer he had spent in Maine and about his adventures in the navy. About Marvin Lampert, a physics student from the Bronx, who had taught him to love music.

"At Columbia," he said, "the top floor of Livingston Hall was filled with physicists and they all loved music."

"That's understandable," she said.

He recounted how his cousin Lily's husband Howard hanged himself and wondered while he was telling her why he was telling her that.

There were all those things he could not, dared not, say about how much he wished he'd known her sooner. Known her when there was more time. How he wanted to know how she was then, and at all times other than then. What he could never now know no matter how much she told him. For words could never bring her to him as she was at all those other times and could not ever be again.

How much he wanted to tell her about himself and he did try and always failed because his words, but not just his words, his efforts to fathom or to remember who or what he was then or at any other time always fell short and he found it was impossible to give himself to her as he so very much wanted to do.

And so in the end there was just the present moment and who they were just then and he was, he thought, so miserably inadequate.

It was dawn when he let himself into the apartment. Under the yellow bedlamp light, the crown of his wife's head was a polished chestnut.

"You're still up."

"You might have called."

"I didn't know you were back in New York."

"I said I'd return Saturday morning. It's Saturday. Or, rather, yesterday was."

"I forgot. Sorry."

"Your surgery is on Monday. That's tomorrow, you know."

"I know. I was with Vera. We were talking."

"Vera? *Armand's* Vera?"

"It's over with Armand."

"I know."

"Go to sleep, Carla."

He needed to find his boxes. Papers, notebooks. Journals and diaries from college, from the navy, from his trip to Normandy. Descriptions of cathedrals in the manner of Henry James. Letters from the German woman. He'd almost married her. He read each one.

Another box. Poems and essays he'd written in his twenties. He sat in the living room reading them aloud. A worn first edition of the poems of Gerard Manley Hopkins. A woman had given him that. Elizabeth. When he was an intern.

"Evening strains to be time's vast,
Womb-of-all, home-of-all, hearse-of-all night."

He rose and walked through the room where his wife lay sleeping. In their bathroom, his leather Dopp kit sat open in the linen closet. He would need a fresh supply of razors. Mouthwash. There were ample Percocets in the orange vial. He yanked a canvas zippered bag from the top shelf.

His navy cotton robe, freshly laundered pajamas. . . Underwear, socks, slippers. . .Sweatpants, a Lacoste shirt, a cardigan. . .The collected poems, first edition.

Twenty-seven.

After a week, Carla brought him back to the apartment overlooking the park. One hand gripped the canvas straps of his zippered bag while the other clutched his wool scarf close about his throat. January-thin rays of light glinted off the snow, making it whiter, colder. He had lived.

He paused in the foyer, taking in what he knew had been his home for almost thirty years. Shelves crammed with books, small round tables, ovals and rectangles, sofas, little objects accumulated in travels. They might have been relics in the vitrines of some anthropological museum. Shimmering with intimations of roles they had played, ways they had served in lives now past, lives one could only guess at. A *moire* evening gown in *Les Invalides* is recognizable as the gown of the Empress Josephine. One knows how it was fastened, and on what sorts of occasions it was worn. But one does not know enough. The details one wants are not provided. He had been irrevocably severed from his former knowledge of things.

He let his wife take his topcoat from him and set his bag down at the harpsichord, staring across to the window and on to the park beyond. The window, the park itself were so much smaller than he remembered. And faded, somehow greyed. In Cardiac Intensive Care, perhaps, one sees larger things, more vivid things. Perhaps that was it.

In the mirror before him, an obscene wine-colored scab wended its way through the stubble that had been his chest hair. He could recall halving a game hen with a heavy knife through the soft rib bones. Or steadying a lobster on his plate for the same deft stroke. He backed away slightly and lowered his eyes to take in the fuller view. On his right leg, another long, jagged line. The same burgundy color, but a thinner, less certain line. His pubic hair was gone. Like a young boy, he thought. And then he reconsidered. A humiliating baldness. The baldness of French girls found sleeping with Nazis.

"You look very well," Vera said when she came to meet him in the lobby of the Gramercy Park Hotel. "I should have had my taxi pick you up. That was thoughtless of me. You really shouldn't be out yet, breathing such cold air."

"I've only come around the corner," he told her. "I *can* walk, you know." She was bundled in a grey mohair coat the color of her eyes. He had never before seen such glow in that particular color.

"It's too cold out. I really should have come for you," she said. "I'm sorry."

"It's wonderful to see you," he said. A phrase that trips from the tongue so readily, that is heard so habitually, its truth value is never in issue. But, Nathan reflected, it was *true*. It *was* wonderful to see her. And to be seen by her. Held fast in that unequivocal, wholly scrutable gaze. It really was absolutely wonderful.

"Come again on Wednesday," he pleaded as she rose to leave. "We'll walk around the park. My first outing."

"You did it!" she cried and hugged him at the end of their walk.

"*You* did it," he told her. He felt suddenly giddy and sobered himself. "I'm not letting anyone help me, you know. They all want to mix in and I just don't want it. But I could not have walked in this cold without you."

"You must let people help, Nathan," she said.

"Well," he said, "it's not like me to depend on others. But I can lean on you, Vera. I don't know why. Strange, really. I hardly know you. I hope you'll come back and walk around the park with me again."

"Day after tomorrow," she said.

As they walked through the Museum of Modern Art, he took her arm and spoke to her of Manet's uses of the color red.

"It saves him from sentimentality," she agreed.

They found themselves in the photography wing.

"I've never much cared for photography," he said.

"Never liked the portraits. I don't like snapshots, either. Never could tell why."

"I don't like them either," she said. "They're dead."

"How do you mean, 'dead?'"

"A photograph freezes its subjects, don't you think? No matter how naturalistic, photographs are always unnatural, dead. Frozen in time, frozen in space. They give me the willies."

"But here is a child going by on a bicycle," he said. "You can see it moving. It's very much alive."

"But it's a moment that has passed," she said. "The photograph attempts to hold that moment in place. Motion never really looks like that."

"I suppose that's true," he said. "Still, death is not the subject matter."

"What I meant," she continued, "is that regardless of subject matter, a photograph's resemblance to experience calls attention to the poignant differences. For the subject of the photograph, the moment is gone. The photographer imprisons that moment when it really wants to flee. He just can't let it pass. Even family snapshots are overlaid by melancholy, nostalgia for the moment that has passed. I always feel a tinge of sadness on everything a camera captures."

They returned to the main exhibition rooms.

"Painted portraits," he said, "of people who have died. Shouldn't you include them in your necrology as well?"

"That's not it at all," she said. She was annoyed with him. "A painting is always fresh and new. From its inception, it is something other than its subject."

"I'm not sure it's such a simple distinction," Nathan said. He had stopped studying the pictures and was watching her instead. Rapt, pondering, her eyebrows knit deeply. There *was* a difference, he decided. Something fresh, new-born in a painting.

Vera, he decided, was undoubtedly a painting. And I, he concluded, I. . . am a photograph.

Colby, he recalled, had startled him once. The way he

seemed to envy women. But I *do* envy *her*, Nathan thought. I could, if she stayed around perhaps, become more like her, more. . .like a painting. For one flickering moment, Nathan considered that he might begin it all again. It is undoubtedly my last opportunity, he thought.

A heart mending, and his patients grateful for his return. Wanting him to know it caused them concern. Pleased to hear his anecdotes again. They reassured each other. "Take good care of yourself, now," they said. "We missed you, you know."

"I'm going to be good as new," he said. "You take care of *your*self."

The congenial little squeaks of Doris Needham's crepe-soled shoes along the office corridors. Department meetings, Heaney's endless droning, endearing for its familiarity. Rounds with residents, their eagerness to see what he saw when he peered through his loops, wanting his vision of things. Peekskill and its immutable lake. Carla: subdued, obliging, and still radiant, somehow. His daughters and their friends. He loved their friends visiting. A raw rush in his veins when they stayed to dinner.

And Vera. Luminous, complicated, miraculous as a snowflake.

Twenty-eight.

The present nastiness, Nathan later recalled, had started with Tom Szabo. With Tom, expansive as ever, extending a warm, dry palm to draw him into an embrace. Tom's other hand grasped the shoulder of a short, damp, ruddy-faced man. "This is Leon Sinrich," Tom had said. "Leon's a terrific guy. You have to get to know him. He's an accountant. Specializes in doctors. Nathan," he'd told the red face, "is an ophthalmologist. Also one helluva guy. Nathan," he had said, "is my best friend."

It had struck Nathan as very odd to hear he was Tom's best friend. He had, for the first time in perhaps several years, wondered if Tom was still at it with Carla. He had long ago let all that pass.

Tom had thought Nathan should meet with Sinrich to find out what the new federal regulations would mean for his business. Nathan no longer got annoyed at Tom referring to his practice as a business, something Nathan knew it definitely was not. He'd gotten past all that, too. But it had struck him as very odd to hear that he was Tom's best friend.

It was Tom who had set Leon Sinrich on him. And Leon would linger in his newly-renovated office, smiling back at him from the celadon enamel coating on all that expensive new equipment. It was Leon's face that would surface on the bills Doris Needham so meticulously prepared and presented for review. Leon said the new regulations placed a ceiling on what he could charge, a ceiling so low he might not be able to breathe in the air remaining beneath. It could not be gotten around, Leon said. Medicare patients would be forbidden from offering more in payment. "Of course you," the disagreeable face continued, "will be profoundly affected since, as I estimate it, eighty percent of your practice is Medicare. Cataracts, degenerative disorders. Am I correct?"

Nathan's lids hung low over his eyes and his chin rested on his chest. He wanted Sinrich to leave. He wanted to take a nap. He could not appreciate Tom's kindness just then.

"What it really cuts into," Sinrich continued, "is your surgery billings. I imagine they support the rest of your operation. I figure your malpractice premium alone at around nineteen, twenty grand."

He certainly knew what he was talking about. Tom always found good people, Nathan recalled.

"So," Sinrich went on, "you have to clear over two hundred just to meet expenses. I don't see that happening."

Celadon, Nathan realized, could be a sickening shade of green.

"You'll have to triple your load, turn them over six an hour. Join a group, an HMO. Or, hire a P.R. firm and. . . ."

Nathan held up his hand. "Enough," he said. "The practice of medicine isn't something you hawk on the street. It's an art. It's not like accounting."

"I'm trying to be realistic with you," Sinrich said.

"I know," Nathan replied. "I'm sorry."

Sinrich laughed. "You medical men are all unrealistic," he said. "That's how I make a living."

It wasn't Sinrich's fault, Nathan knew. But his professional life was being overlaid with a thick coat of anxiety, a coat he knew he would not be able to shake even after Sinrich was gone. And he could not forget it had been Tom who had so generously arranged this meeting. Once again, he found himself wondering if Tom and Carla were still at it.

She had never spoken of Tom after that day in Truro, but he could not ignore the changes in his wife over the last few years. How clarified, how resolute, how self-possessed she had become. A zealousness about her work, it was impossible not to notice. And she was now, well, a *phenom* of sorts at some downtown gallery. Perhaps her ardor was fueled by what she shared with Tom. Or perhaps she was flourishing because Tom had vanished. It might be either way; Nathan had no way of knowing which it was.

It was, in fact, Time more than anything else. It was, in some measure, Felix's apology, which she had not understood at the time. It was also, in great measure, Lisle. Lisle grew angrier as she matured but, to Carla's dismay, refused to leave home. She wanted something from her mother before she could leave, and she persisted, taunting, prodding, demanding something Carla could not provide. Her peachy cheeks inflamed with wrath, her blonde hair damp on her forehead, her eyes would burn. "I hate you," Lisle would cry out. "You're such a. . .a nothing!"

And then, one autumn, it seemed it was time. Time to tell Tom that his thoughtlessness pained her, that the futility of their arrangement pained her, that she was tired of the pain. It was time to forsake the parties that brought her so much admiration, that caused people to say what a superb caterer she might be.

One autumn evening, Carla tore apart the clay figure she was dawdling over in the studio at the Lexington Avenue Y and began feverishly, unfalteringly, to remake it. Tools she had obediently used for their specified purposes were set out in their usual places at her bench. But she took them into her hands with reverence and awe, as if she were receiving a just-born infant. She dug and clawed at the figure on its wire armature, elongated its hands, its neck, thickened its feet, hollowed its cheeks.

George, the janitor, told her he had to close, he had to get on home. "I'll lock up," she said. She pleaded with him. "I have to keep at this," she said. It was time.

Nathan had no inkling of the processes by which his wife had become a sculptor. He had no idea how things stood with Tom. He knew only that it was Tom who had sent Leon Sinrich into his office and he knew that Leon would, henceforth, sit on his shoulder like some warty toad.

He remembered something his father was fond of saying: Every day every man must swallow a toad. Leon would be his daily bitter draught.

So much more was he grateful for Vera.

Twenty-nine.

As Nathan's heart healed and his body felt more itself, he found new and various ways in which Vera could make him stronger.

In early March, he asked if she would help him revive his tennis game, return the balls, slowly, gently. She obliged, and soon he was teaching her to gauge the distance to a backhand, to step into her forehand, to bring her full weight down on her serve.

"You're doing so well with your tennis," he told her then, "I'd love to teach you to ski as well. I can't keep up with Alex and Lisle anymore. You'd be a good skier. I'm sure of it."

"I really don't think I can learn at my age," she said.

"Nonsense," he said. "You're not your age, Vera. The rules don't apply to you."

He took her to a fine, glowing shop on Madison Avenue. "Bogner," he told her, "is the very finest."

She attended carefully to his instructions and cut a sure, graceful path down the beginners' slope. Nathan beamed with pride as he watched her, the shiny dark braid flying out behind her.

"I told you the rules don't apply to you, " he said.

He led her to the chair lift at the foot of the smallest mountain. She shrank back against him.

"I can't," she said.

Nathan put his arm about her. Within the puffy jacket, her small, uncertain frame. "C'mon," he said, "hold onto me."

The pulley stopped and the little chair swung on its wire. Vera gripped the handrail tightly and bit her lip. "We're almost at the top," Nathan said. "Just slide off the seat with your skis on the ground."

He edged her off the chair and helped her to her feet.

"I can't ski down," she said. "It's much too steep."

"This is the only way down," he said gently. "Just follow me and do as I say."

At the foot of the mountain, Vera unbuckled her boots.

"You must go up again," Nathan said. "Right now. And again after that until you get used to it. You're doing very well."

On the lift, she closed her eyes and buried her head in his shoulder. A small bird trembling against him.

On the trail that led back to the pro shop, she paused to watch the rosy children shussing and tumbling on the beginner slope. "I wish I'd learned when _I_ was a child," she said wistfully.

Nathan could scarcely draw breath, his throat had tightened so. Holding her in the lift chair, he had thought of another rosy child, of Lisle when she was young. Of Lisle when *he* was young. At that moment when the pulley stopped, he was a man whose heart had never lain in a box of ice. He was a man who was strong and young and it was, at that moment, such a long time ago.

Woman, girl, the transmutations of gypsy magic. She coaxed him to a discotheque, the sort of place he'd never conceived. Once more, the raised eyebrows widening her eyes, the mischievous shrug of her shoulders, the throaty giggle as she urged him onto the crowded floor. Her wavy dark hair, set free at last, cascaded over her shoulders, undulating with the movements of her body. Sure, sensual pulsings, captivating him, embarrassing him. Her arms were raised above her head, her torso swaying, her feet barely touching the floor as her weight shifted rapidly from one to the other. She beckoned with long fingers he was certain could reach inside him and, when he pursued her, awkward and hesitant, she chucked him under the chin and swirled about him again. Soon he'd reworked some old dance steps to the disco beat and improvised a lighthearted movement for his arms. He was drawn by the game, the pounding music, the flashing lights. He looked across at her. Tiny beads of perspiration on her upper lip, strands of dark hair across her forehead. They might have been alone on the dance floor.

He was growing weary, his breath coming in short, insufficient gasps. He was afraid to tell her.

She looked into his face, her own damp and beaming. She stopped her dance and threw her arms about him, kissing him on the cheek. "Thanks for the dance," she said. "I think we've done enough, don't you?"

She would always know him, Nathan thought, always anticipate him.

It had been like making love. He confessed to himself it was not the first time he had thought of her that way. He wondered if he might approach her. She was, after all, free. And for all her bounty, she was a woman alone with two sons, a woman in need of sheltering, the woman who had wanted to marry Armand. He wondered what he might say to turn things that way.

But he was, he reflected, a convalescent. It had been an evening's adventure, he told himself at last. A marvelous adventure, an exploration of the limits of what was possible. That's what this friendship with Vera is, he concluded: A journey to the limits of what is possible.

It was almost April, the much-awaited month that never keeps its appointment. March will never conclude, Nathan thought. He despised his topcoat. "Wearying," he called it.

Vera followed him up the ruby-carpeted steps to the mezzanine of the Metropolitan Opera. He glanced back as he spoke, gesturing and calling out above the din of the milling audience. He wanted her to appreciate *Don Giovanni*, to understand why it was surely Mozart's greatest opera.

When they reached their seats, she shed her coat and stood wedged between the rows, smiling down at him. A smile he had never seen on her before. Beneath the smile, a round collar of thick French lace. Old-fashioned puffed sleeves were bordered by the same lace. And the rest was black velvet, gathered thickly at a dropped waist and flowing, Nathan surmised, to some point just above her ankles. It was all held shut by a vertical row of sparkling jet beads that scattered light maddeningly and that ran the length of the dress from the lace at her throat fully down to the hem. It was a little girl's dress except for those jet buttons. Those buttons, Nathan decided, made all the difference.

He could not have said how it happened that he reached for her hand, how she closed hers over his and somehow drew it into her lap. But the last act was half over and the great statue, bathed in crimson light, would soon appear from below the stage and his right hand was in her lap and the buttons, somehow, were undone so that his hand slipped across the velvet and fell below to thighs as smooth as bone.

"My God, Vera! You've nothing on!"

She shrugged and turned partly toward him, a glint in her eye.

He withdrew his hand brusquely but as he did so his fingertips grazed some lushly tufted shrub. He buried the fugitive hand in his other and straightened in his seat. The damp on his fingers warmed, then vaporized.

Peonies, they were. Carmine and rose, their centers all bronzy gold. Multifoliate ranunculae, musky full blossoms blown toward him. He did not see the red-lit statue emerge onto the stage. He saw Vera, splayed among feather beds, heady as a peony in June. And he wanted to rub his face in her, to breathe her. He wanted, quite simply, to smell her.

They were silent as they left and very still as they waited for his car to be brought around.

"Vera," he said when they were inside it, "I'm scarred and shaven. Bristly and shorn. You'll find me very ugly."

She took his hand and again she smiled. An utterly new smile, one he'd only just seen for the first time that evening.

It's true, Nathan concluded. She *does* anticipate my every thought.

Thirty.

An eager, somewhat unctuous, young man named Jordan Avery answered Nathan's notice in the hospital bulletin. He was just starting out and a single examining room plus a shared receptionist seemed exactly right.

"Everyone," he told Nathan, "holds you in such high esteem. I'd be honored to share an office with a senior member of the faculty."

Nathan had merely hoped for help meeting expenses. He had viewed Avery as a refuge from the insistent croakings of Sinrich's warty toad. But now, here was an avid admirer, a cornucopia of compliments.

Jordan Avery set out on his desk a colored snapshot of

his baby son in a lavish brass frame. He strode through the office with a quick smart step and suggested to Doris Needham that she really ought to put the files on computer disks. He bought her a fax machine as a present. Nathan told him as politely as he could manage that his patients were accustomed to bills typed on his letterhead by Mrs. Needham in digits they could feel with their fingertips, not that they needed to do so. He said Mrs. Needham knew where all the files were and that there was plenty of room for them now that the celadon enameled cabinets were in place. And, he told Avery, Mrs. Needham had no real use for a fax machine.

"The office you saw is the office you rented," he told Avery. He put a fatherly arm about the young man and took him to dine at The Oyster Bar.

"Medicine is an art," he said, picking clean one delicate smelt after another. "You don't want your patients seeing you as yet another machine. You don't want them thinking this is yet another greedy business." The younger man nodded gravely. "We're men of medicine," Nathan continued. "A science, yes. But also an art. A humane art with a hallowed tradition, an ancient prestige. You want a very human setting here. Human in the classic sense, if you know what I mean."

Some months later, Jordan Avery took Nathan to dinner. Art-deco sconces, peach-colored walls. On each dish, little curls of vegetables Nathan could not identify. The patrons carried slim briefcases and their laughter was like new wine. Not one of them, it seemed, was a day older than Nathan's daughter.

Avery produced a manila envelope and spilled its contents onto the table. Bates Associates, it said. Consultants to the Medical Profession. Nathan flicked some shredded radish to the side of his plate. The woman at the table just ahead, he noticed, had pale bobbed hair that moved like liquid.

"They make a videotape of us talking about glaucoma," Avery was saying. "We play it on a monitor in the waiting room. A loop that plays continuously. Seeing us on television reinforces confidence. Our patients see us as celebrities."

The morsel of blackened snapper Nathan had speared on his fork dropped into the little dish of red sauce on his plate. "A monitor," he said. "And a loop."

"And they do a quarterly mailing. Newsletter thing. *Eye Services Update* or whatever. Photos of us and stories about our new techniques and the superb results we're achieving. They send it to all our patients and, for a few dollars more, they can track the zip codes that show up most often on our list and saturate those areas. All computerized."

"Saturate," Nathan said. "That's really something." He ordered some more wine. Avery, he suddenly realized, wore French cuffs. He hated French cuffs. And big vulgar cufflinks. Like the brass on that picture frame.

Carla traveled to Florida often now to tend to her mother. Several days each month. At first, this new routine left Nathan unanchored, abandoned. But his resentment soon faded as he came to comprehend the possibilities this arrangement afforded.

"There'll be a fireplace in our room and a view of the slopes," Nathan told Vera one early December day. "And we'll stay for two nights, Friday and Saturday. The whole weekend."

"Ah," they said when the porter let them into their room. An ample, spice-scented armoire. The fruity perfume of bath foam. Nathan stretched himself out on the bed and ran through the numbers on the television control. Blades of grass rendered viscous by a photographer's long lens.

"The mantis's brain," a satiny voice told him, "secretes a hormone during intercourse that prevents ejaculation. To have her eggs fertilized, the female must first bite off the head of her mate, stemming the flow of the hormone, thus permitting ejaculation to occur."

"He dies in both senses of the word," Nathan said.

"Some folks just have to lose their heads a bit before they can come," Vera said. Opalescent florets of foam slid down her legs and vanished into the carpet.

"Besides everything else, Vera, you're very funny," he said. "You make up jokes like that right on the spot. I can only tell jokes I've read or heard from someone else."

"Your remark about dying was very clever," she said.

"Oh, a dry little pun. You, on the other hand, are always surprising."

"But you remember jokes and you tell them so well," she said. "And all those limericks. They're very funny." She had wrapped a thick white towel into a turban around her head and another served as a sarong. She sat, yoga-style, at the foot of the bed. "How about a massage?" she said.

"No thanks," he said. "I have to admit, they make me uncomfortable." He muted the volume on the television. "Where do your jokes come from?" He was sombre now. He yearned for something, some thing of hers he could not name.

Vera sensed his mood and thought carefully. "I think a joke disorders the world in some way," she said. "Reveals the incongruous or the irrational in the world. It's irreverence, I think. A certain disrespect for order."

"Women don't usually make jokes the way you do," he said.

"I suppose it's not ladylike to be so disrespectful."

"Is that why I can't make up jokes? Am I too respectful of the order in things?"

"You're very reluctant to disturb the *status quo,* Nathan."

"You mean I'm a coward."

"I mean you seem to want to make things stand still and behave. Pitting yourself against the processes of time, against disruptions and the quotidian derangements of things. Spontaneous eruptions are what *I* love. But they really unnerve you, I think."

"It's true what you say. I don't like disruption. But I want to learn, Vera. Can you teach me to make up jokes? I want to bravely disarrange things."

"It's not bravery," she said. "The world is already deranged. The thing is to observe it without rushing in to straighten it all out. Just accept it and laugh."

"Acceptance," he said. "I'm not very good at that either."

He sat up and leaned toward her, reached for her hand and uncoiled her across the bed. He uncoiled the white towels, the sarong, the turban. They lay thick and thirsty across the newly-laundered bedsheets. Soft, gauzy linens. White linens. White towels. Vera uncoiled. He pushed his fingers through her hair and full, clear drops of water fell upon the linen. Thirst. Thirst. Whiteness. And thirst.

It was when Vera slept, her wiry legs entwined in his, their feet nesting one in the other, her black hair unbraided, spilling over pillows and the blanket's border, over his arm wrapped about her, when he saw how soundly she slept held close this way, how naturally it came to her, how easily she meshed her limbs with his, that he knew his life had entirely missed its point. For he could never doze, could never close an eye with anyone, even Vera, so close by. And so he held her through the night, thinking how lucky he was. How rich she was, a deep and endless well; but also a bright, darting light, inventing itself at every moment. In her need for him, she invigorated him in the most powerful way. These thoughts filled him with amazement and gratitude as he clung to her, waiting for morning.

Immortality, Robin Colby had said, is what all men crave. It is, Colby seemed certain, what a man finds in a woman if she is kept at the proper distance. Nathan wondered as he wrapped himself about Vera, pressing against her as she slept, if she was, in fact, at the proper distance. He knew he had never come so close to death as when, almost a year ago, his chest had been cut open, Taylor and his team peering mercilessly into it. And there was no doubt, Nathan thought, that he had never come so close to life as on these early mornings, holding in his own bare arms this supple woman who was, at any moment, as much a girl as a woman.

Would she, he wondered, lose her miraculous powers if she were promised to him until he died? If he married her, if she were to be there at his deathbed? He wondered if that would alter her.

No, Nathan thought that night in the fruit-scented room at the foot of the ski slope, best to keep things as they are. What Colby would call an *idée fixe.*

In the morning, he boarded the gondola to Alpenhaus, a gathering spot near the top of the most challenging trail. He ordered a double vodka martini, very dry. Gaily-colored tassled hats, plump mittens. Robust, cold-pricked faces. Congenial talk.

On the crusty white crest, Nathan planted his poles and pushed off. The narrow slope soon levelled onto a plateau. His breath was short and the cold sheared his lungs and his throat. A newsletter! A newsletter? Did he really imagine I would advertise? Jordan Avery will be out on his ear, he decided. He will be out in the street with his fax machine and his tasteless brass picture frame and his cufflinks. Out by the first of the year. "I can *not* accept such disarrangements," he said to a passing clump of hemlocks. "I'm just not a very accepting sort of man."

"I'm hungry," Vera announced when they were finally in the car heading south on Sunday afternoon.

"It's almost four," he said. "Let's wait until we get to Peekskill."

"Peekskill? We can't go there. Carla will be home by now."

Nathan lowered his head and slurred his words. "Carla's having some people over tonight and we're very late getting back. I really can't take you into the City and return to Peekskill in time. I thought I would drop you in Peekskill. At the station. You could take the train to New York."

He slouched down into his collar but Vera's eyes were everywhere. They tore at his face. "Nathan, we need to talk," she said.

"Vera, darling, don't spoil a nice weekend. It really is quite late. And it has been a lovely time."

Still she filled the car.

"Sunday dinner, Vera. You *know* I have to be there for

occasions like that. You're the one I care about. Really, Vera, you know it's true." He'd become a pedlar, niggardly and feral.

When Vera finally spoke again, her words were clipped, her husky voice strangely icy. "This is not acceptable," she said. "I really can't continue this way. Think it over, Nathan. Think it over carefully and let me know."

Carla used those very words when he called her from a diner along the highway. "Be reasonable, Carla," he said. "I came up to the Berkshires this morning for a bit of skiing and now the road's all frozen over. I need to stay here until it's plowed."

"This is not the arrangement," she said. "How do I face the guests alone? What do I tell them?"

"Tell them the truth," he said. "Tell them the road is frozen over."

"I can't continue this way, Nathan," she told him. "I think you'd better consider what you're doing."

It was close to midnight when he returned to the drafty house. His wife's right hand zigzagged over the Sunday puzzle, making little marks with a thin blue pen. The fingers of her left hand absently tested the temperature in her coffee cup. Nathan could see the remains of a baked ham and a crystal bowl half full of limp salad on the counter behind her.

"I'm terribly sorry about dinner," he began.

Carla did not look up. "Tom and Tilly took their kids skiing this morning," she said. "In the Berkshires. *They* got home in time. This is not the arrangement, Nathan. I'm not going to continue this way."

There was no fat, no sinew, no flesh at all on Nathan's bones. They were windbeaten and desiccated. Even his tongue was a stone in his mouth and his mouth was a dry, stale nut.

Thirty-one.

There were small things that happened before he lost Vera. Small things along the way. These things might have happened differently, but losing Vera was, he finally knew, something that would inevitably have happened. They had explored the far reaches of conceivable configurations and throughout she'd given him proof that it was all entirely possible. The impossibility, he finally understood, was an impossibility in him. And so he understood his loss as something of his own making, something that flowed from his own nature, and his grief would not abate.

The evening of Nina Phillips's fiftieth birthday was one of those things along the way. It was Valentine's Day. Carla had sculpted a fat ceramic cupid as a gift.

"It's absolutely wonderful," Lisle told Nathan. "Its penis came off in the firing and Mom reattached it with a tiny screw. Now you can have it on or off, depending on who's coming for dinner. Perfect for Nina, isn't it?"

"It's atrocious," Nathan told them both. "Give Nina my best because this is one birthday party I won't be attending."

Alex found him asleep in his favorite chair when she returned home. "It sounds pretty awful," she said when Nathan told her about the cupid.

"Alex," he said suddenly, "you know Vera Lenz. Armand's friend?"

"Yes."

"She's my friend, too."

"Yes," she said. "I know."

"I'd like you to meet her. With me, I mean. It's Friday and Vera will be lighting candles. There'll be challah and kosher wine. I love being at Vera's on Friday nights. Please come along with me tonight."

After Vera was gone, he would find there was one image he could not erase: Vera, her face glowing like wheat as she lit and blessed the candles. Her long fingers across the flames, a conjurer, beckoning the fragrant tallow smoke,

The Speed of Light

summoning ancient spirits of comfort and peace. Vera, potent in her wisdom of ages, her two sons who knew all this, respectful and loving. They felt blessed by her as he did.

He had often been drawn by those flames, phoning to ask her to dinner, knowing she would say it was *shabbos* and that he was welcome at her table. How he loved to spend a Friday evening sipping the sweet wine, savoring the golden bread dunked in rich broth. Yet, even at her table, he was an orphan peering through a window at some bountiful family feast, wishing he could truly partake. Something kept him apart, however. That same invisible bar that had kept him from the warmth of Felix's embrace. The mysterious blessings she chanted in Hebrew connected Vera to the miraculous, transported her sons with her to somewhere Nathan could not go. This vision of Vera, wrapped as it was in so powerful a longing, he would never dispel that.

"You're so happy when you're with her," Alex told him as they drove home. "You should marry her, Daddy. You deserve to be happy."

"Ah, sweetheart," he said, scrubbing her tight, red curls. "It's not so simple as you imagine."

"How was the party?" he asked his wife when she returned home.

"I enjoyed it," she said, "but it wasn't your sort of thing."

She was a thoroughbred, his wife. A woman of great restraint. But Nathan could see that the character bred into her was eroding, ebbing out of her and muddying those aquamarine eyes.

The evening at Marvin Lampert's was the last of those things along the way. It had not been noted on his calendar. Not on the one Doris Needham kept.

"You should have told Doris," he had said to Carla. "It's the only calendar I attend to."

"It's here on the big calendar in the kitchen," she said. "Circled in red. You can't miss it."

"I never look in the kitchen," he said. "For anything."

He'd reserved a table by the dance floor that evening at the Rainbow Room. He loved dancing with Vera. He was planning to wear the Dusseldorf tuxedo once again. A celebration of sorts. One year since their evening at _Don Giovanni_.

"But these are brilliant, interesting people," Carla said. "A gala at the Rockefeller University mansion. Can you really think of not going?" Her voice was brittle, weary.

"These are the best people we know," he told Vera sheepishly. "Tomorrow night, darling, the dance floor will still be there."

"It was you who taught me to love Bach," he told Marvin Lampert. "You and the physicists in Livingston Hall." He was mouthing the words, the click of the telephone receiver at Vera's end still echoing in his head.

"We were children then," Lampert said. He dabbed his heavy lips with a linen napkin. "Now that the universe is so beyond comprehension, Bach seems naive, doesn't he?"

"Not at all," Nathan said. "He's so complex! Music addressed to God. The intricate, orderly universe." He had to labor over words that he expected would slide from his tongue. He was not thinking about music. He was thinking that he would leave his wife. That he would run to Vera and tell her he had thought it over. He would tell her he had decided.

"We were naive," Lampert was saying. "God, or Nature, or whatever you want to call it, isn't merely complex. It's utterly unresolved. Sometimes I think continuity is nothing more than a scientist's dream. The world I contend with is one disjuncture after another."

"More like Mahler," Stew Abrams suggested.

"Worse," Lampert said. "More like John Cage."

"I never imagined _you'd_ come to that," Nathan said. It

seemed Lampert had betrayed him. Or perhaps the betrayer was Bach. It no longer mattered. He would be done with this arrangement of things. He would begin now bravely disarranging them. There was still a chance, a life that sparkled. Disarranged. Deranged. Yes, he thought, definitely more like John Cage.

"*I* still love Bach," Maxene Abrams whispered as they said good night. It had been her toe along his leg at dinner.

He hurried to phone Vera. He shifted his weight from one foot to the other and counted ten rings. He hung up and called the floral delivery. "Anemones," he said. "Enough anemones to fill a room." He never did discover what became of those anemones.

Telegrams and more calls. Letters that received no reply. The custodian at the preschool refused him access. Now, he could think of nothing else.

He paid a visit to Lily's brother, Gerald. I want a divorce, is what he planned to say. I am a free man, is what he imagined writing to Vera. Long corridors of cherrywood panels hung with large paintings. Originals, Nathan noted. Gerald had done well for himself.

But Gerald's face was the color of rotting fruit, and he growled belligerently into a speaker on his telephone. Nathan counted three other voices in the conversation.

"How many lawyers are involved in one divorce?" he asked when Gerald hung up.

His cousin shook his head and drew a vial of pills from his drawer. "Complicated mess, this one," he said. He swallowed a few tablets. "They're all messy, of course. *Mine* is messy. My partner is handling it for me and I'm still going to lose my shirt. Divorce stinks. Always stinks."

"Yes," Nathan agreed.

Nathan asked about Gerald's sons and about his tennis.

"Don't play much," Gerald said. "Heart," he said. "How's yours?"

Nathan said his tennis was okay and that he was hoping

177

one of Gerald's partners might look over the pension plan he'd set up for Mrs. Needham. Gerald said he'd put some-one right on it. Nathan wished him good luck with his divorce and said good bye.

And then his darkness returned. Deserts of no identifi-able color. Shrill keenings of animals too famished to eat. Interminable ululations of nocturnal creatures inhabiting his skull, his jaws. Until morning, he let them cry their hungry cries.

This tenebrous vat became his domicile. He no longer expected connections with things; he expected isolating fog as one expects a certain odor upon returning home. Two fifty-three, two fifty-four, red numerals on his clock blink-ing like rats' eyes in the night. Crumpled bedlinen, morning nausea were as familiar to him as the backs of clenched teeth to an unslept tongue.

In time, it was no longer Vera so much as her legacy. She had unveiled his abyss and he loathed himself. Were she to return, it could not heal him, could not complete him. It was not that he wanted to have her back so much as that he wanted, somehow, to become her. TO BE HER.

To be her? A woman? Was it possible? Was it possible, as she sometimes seemed to demonstrate, that *anything* was possible? Could he really want to *be* her? Was it possible to want that and, if that were possible, was it, in fact, possible to be her? Or was he wanting the impossible? It seemed possible sometimes. In the darknesses of winter and the shorter bitter nights of April. In the dark light of July and the steaming darks of August.

"We are like a child," he read in September, "who holds in his hand a sunbeam."

It had really been too hot, too sticky to play tennis and the persistent little tightnesses in his chest had begged for his attention but he had slipped furtively out of his navy blazer and into his tennis whites. He had had, he remem-bered later that evening, some misgivings about playing on

Yom Kippur. But he had wanted a chance to play singles with Tom. A chance to beat him as he had in the old days. To beat him in spite of the little tightnesses. In spite of that killer serve.

And now there was a tennis ball lodged in his chest. A hard round knot in his chest. Tom's serve was making its way through. And in the blue bedroom his wife, wrapped in her rose-printed gown, kept entirely to her side of the imaginary line down the center of their bed.

He woke from his troubled sleep. The book he had been reading lay on the floor. The coral impatiens on the terrace straightened on their stems. The air coming through the French doors now was cooler and dryer than it had been all day. He let his head fall backward and resumed his dream. Something larger than a bullet, smaller than a fist, was stuck in his chest. The man who had made love to Carla all these years, the man who had sent Leon Sinrich to sit on his shoulder, had sent a tennis ball right into him.

It was merely angina. It would pass. He bent over and picked up his book. The letters grew large and then small on the page. He wanted to throw up. He stepped out onto the terrace and studied the buildings south of Gramercy Park. The windows were white splotches in the dampness. It would be embarrassing showing up at the hospital. They would ask why he'd waited so long. He would wake his wife. She would drive.

Thirty-two.

The Doctors Berg had an office in the same building as Nathan. He'd seen their names on the directory in the lobby. Husband and wife ophthalmologists, like the Colbys. And now they were in his office inquiring about his health.

"Left anterior descending, I would imagine," Mordecai Berg was saying. Brenda Berg shifted her eyes from her husband to Nathan and regarded him with immense sympathy.

"Yes, that was it," Nathan said briskly, "but I'm fine now. Very nice of you to drop by. Really very nice."

"Vultures," he told Doris Needham when they were gone. "Perched up there on the fourteenth floor, waiting to devour my practice. Can't even let the carrion cool. That's how vultures are, you know. Did you see them salivating over the new equipment?"

Mordecai Berg had left Nathan a dark blue folder containing what he called "a little suggestion."

"Whenever you have a moment to look it over," Brenda Berg had said, "we'll be delighted to talk."

"They want to share my practice for three years and then take it over entirely," he told Doris. "This is my retirement plan, this little blue folder. Courtesy of Mordecai and Brenda Berg. Such kindness!"

He slammed the folder onto Doris' desk and made for the little closet in the powder room. The vodka restored moisture to his mouth.

Now Stew Abrams, Nathan thought as he returned to his consultation room, was never burdened to consider retirement. Stew hit a smashing serve one crisp autumn morning and ran in for the volley. Before he reached the ball, he fell dead on the court. That, Nathan had decided, was the way a heart ought to fail. He had said as much to Maxene. "It's the best way to go," he had said. Then he had remembered the sensation of Maxene's toe against his leg. "Well," he ventured, "the *second* best way."

There are seasons that burst suddenly upon us: a first snowfall, a first daffodil. But autumn seems a more gradual thing. Berries darken, leaves drop, coats on small animals thicken. Yet there are those autumn storms that can tear every leaf from the trees in a single night. Then branches appear startled as new lovers who, riding on passion, shed their clothes all at once and discover themselves too soon naked.

Nathan sometimes thought it was Vera's departure that brought on the storm. As if that could account for his accelerated autumn. But the heart, of course, and its ventricles and plaques and its garland of arteries all have reasons of their own. And once an infarction occurs, it is more than a possibility that it will occur again. The possibility that it might occur on the tennis court. Atop a mountain, possibly. And it was, for the Federal Aviation Agency, a disturbing possibility that it might occur in the cockpit of his Cessna. "The harm that could come to those on the ground," the examiner had said.

Nathan struggled for the appropriate analogy. Losing his pilot's license, selling the plane. It was not like losing a limb or like contracting a crippling disease. It was not like a dishonorable military discharge, although he considered for awhile that it was, in fact, somewhat like that. A public humiliation, he thought. An impeachment is what it most resembled. The examiners had voted "no confidence" and stripped him of his wings. Of his power to flee his wearying fretfulness.

And it did not end there. Armand and Tom, cautioned by the fate of Stew Abrams, declined invitations for tennis. Tom was always busy. Armand's knee was worse than ever. No one, it seemed, would serve the ball that might cause that frangible artery to fail.

It was not so much that he had planned to ski again in Aspen as that it was now forbidden. Entire portions of the globe were forbidden. Only after his visit to Dr. Taylor did he realize how much of the world was so far above sea level. Too much of a risk, Taylor told him. Forbidden.

So was a second cup of coffee. A lamb chop. A runny Brie. "And in bed," Taylor said, "well, I'm sure you know about that."

"Never mind," Nathan told him. "It's the best way to go."

"That's not what I meant," the cardiologist said. "You're taking a beta-blocker. You may experience some difficulty."

Nathan slid down in his chair. "I'm impotent," he mur-

181

mured. It was an incantation he hoped would work an instant antidote.

"What I'm saying," Taylor continued, "is that you may experience some difficulty. We can talk further if you find that you do. We can tinker with the dosage or switch to a different drug."

An accelerated autumn. He was a stark, gnarled branch. All his colored leaves had been ripped away too soon.

January break. It was the warm wedge of winter when his daughters returned from their studies. The obligatory chaos of the holidays was behind them, Carla refurbished the refrigerator daily, he could bask in their company.

Their colleagues came and went, heaping long scarves and secondhand coats in the foyer. A straw-haired Greek who had followed Alexandra home from Italy. Lisle's beau, a voluble architect eleven years her senior. A fine-boned, olive-complected woman with a dancer's calves and opulent spectacles. She inhabited Lisle's room, consuming sprouted peas and scores of novels. There were early morning whispers and the *lento* sonorities of philosophical speculation late into the night. The pale, attenuated Martin, still Alex's closest friend, sat beside her for harpsichord duets. Wittgenstein and Derrida and Paul DeMan. Marguerite Duras and Habermas. They crunched endive and macadamias and drank Cointreau with quinine.

Nathan could not return home early enough, could not live vastly enough. He asked Martin for a good introduction to Deconstructionism and devoured it. Lacan. Lyotard. He wanted to understand, to be included, to face out with them to their wide winter sky.

"I guess I'm retrograde. I must seem bourgeois," he would say when they invited him to join in.

Their voices were fine and light. He wanted to rub against them. He wanted to bury his face in all their shiny hair, in their clavicles, their navels, and inhale.

Thirty-three.

Lily could disappoint him deeply these days if she were not available on Wednesday evenings.

"I wouldn't dismiss Berg's offer out of hand," she told him. She was looking extremely pretty, Nathan thought. Burnished, enhanced by time. Still meticulously groomed, still those neutral shades that blended with her fair complexion to produce the sense of a small furry animal. Still the trim legs, pertly crossed. He realized as he studied her face that he had not expected her to age so well. "It's a perfectly reasonable offer," she continued, "and it's done all the time by healthier physicians than you. You really should consider it."

"For godsake, Lily. My practice is all I have left!"

"Oh, c'mon Nathan. This is the start of a whole new phase, time for the things you've always wanted to do."

"I can't fly anymore. Can't get a tennis game. Can't ski most places. There's nothing else I *can* do, Lily."

"That's not the point," she said. "Now's the time to play the harpsichord, take up photography. Try yoga. Time to do things just for enjoyment, Nathan. Just for fun."

"I know what I enjoy," he said, "and I can't do any of those things. I don't want to learn new things. I wouldn't enjoy *that* at all!"

Lily recrossed her legs, sucked in her lips and studied him. "I suppose that's true, Nathan," she said at last. "You probably wouldn't enjoy that. Perhaps you'd better not think about the Bergs anymore."

Nathan stretched out on the beige sofa and loosened his tie. He looked across at his cousin. When he was fourteen and she was twelve. . . *We have a little sister and she has no breasts.* He had always thought of Lily when he read that.

"You're letting your hair go grey," he said.

"Silver," she said. "Acknowledging my age."

"It's very attractive. I could be aging more gracefully," he sighed, "but it all went at once, Lily. There's nothing left."

"There's plenty left," she said. "You're just refusing to see it. Your family. . ."

"Lily, please!"

"Well, the girls, Nathan. And grandchildren someday."

"Alex and her friends are gorgeous," he agreed. "The best thing I have. But they come and go. And Lisle's always busy at her studio. The girls are wonderful, but they're not my life."

Lily rose from the curvy beige chair and walked to the window where she stood staring down at the street. "We keep avoiding the issue, don't we," she said quietly, not turning to face him. "We never talk about what you really want, about what's been missing all this time."

"Which is?"

She turned and looked directly at him. "A real woman, Nathan. Someone to be close to, to give time to. Someone to give your*self* to. That would be enough, wouldn't it?"

Nathan stared up at the ceiling. The corners of his jaw were heavy, lumpy. "There *was* a woman like that," he began. He shut his eyes and covered them with his hand. "It just wasn't possible," he said finally. "Not possible, that's all."

They left the beige office and turned onto Sixty-third Street, to Lily's favorite restaurant. Nathan ordered Cointreau in quinine.

"Something Alex showed me." A smile that quickly faded.

"You're melancholic," Lily said. His hand was resting on the soft linen tablecloth and she closed hers over it. "More melancholic than usual."

"I've always been afraid I'd end up like my father," he said. "Dry and lifeless. I think it's happened after all."

His cousin pursed her lips and drew her chin back. "You're nothing like him, Nathan. I remember him well. He couldn't enjoy anything. Not music, not laughter. Not a sunny day. You're much more like your mother."

"You know what they always said about me, my father and Irv? They said Mom turned me into a sissy."

"You're a sensitive, cultivated man," Lily said.

"But do you think I'm effeminate?" Nathan was leaning toward her, studying her face for a sign.

Lily raked her fork over her brook trout, pushing the almonds to one side. She looked up at him, her pretty cheekbone resting in her palm, her pale eyes consoling. "That's what you've feared the most, isn't it? That's what you've really been afraid of all these years."

"That's ridiculous," Nathan said.

"Nonetheless. . . . You want some of these almonds?" she said. "They put on too many almonds."

"I don't know what you're talking about," he said. "I just think I've missed out on the juice somehow."

"You've done your best," she said. "Shall we have dessert?"

"Of course, dessert," Nathan said. "I'm not my father, after all."

Lily beckoned the waiter and ordered two *crèmes brûlées*.

"Do you think it's too late for therapy?" Nathan asked.

"It's never a matter of timing," she told him.

"Well, I've started a new affair."

"That's promising."

"Maxene Abrams. I'm sure you've met her. Stew Abrams's widow."

"Now *that's* timing," she laughed.

"Actually," Nathan said, "*she* determined the timing." He cocked his head and looked at her sadly. He lifted his dessert spoon and then set it down again. "I'm impotent, Lily. The medication's left me impotent."

"I don't think therapy is your answer, Nathan."

"Too far gone, huh?"

"I've had men like you as patients," she said. "They spend years wondering what's wrong with everyone else."

"Is it possible my little cousin has become a man-hater?"

"I know *you*, Nathan," she said. "Just change your medication. That's your best bet."

185

"What if it doesn't work?"

"I think it's your best bet, Nathan. I really do."

"And if it doesn't work?"

"Have some *crème brûlée*, Nathan. It's absolutely delicious."

Thirty-four.

There were evenings when he could not say where his wife was. He liked to imagine her at the ceramics studio at the Lexington Avenue "Y". Often enough she was there, he knew, and it was agreeable to think of her there, chatting with other women, hands damp, slathered with clay.

He had, of course, considered other possibilities. He sometimes thought she might be dining with Tom. He had heard they'd been seen together. It did not matter, really; she was entitled. Still, if it were Tom, after all this time. . .

There were evenings, he knew, that she spent at that women's gallery in Soho. Perhaps she was helping a colleague hang a show, perhaps she was setting up a show of her own. Or they might all be gathered in one of those dreadful lofts, talking about art. *Women's* art. It was, apparently, some wholly distinct thing. Louise Bourgeois! Carla had insisted he attend a show of hers. "Penis envy!" he had said, and then left.

One evening he attended an opening of Carla's work. Wood, marble. Materials that needed chipping away. He hadn't thought she had it in her. Young women in black tuxedos, sleek, colorless hair, inscrutable faces. Young men in turtlenecks, the same sleek hair, looking strangely like priests. "You might be the new Louise Bourgeois," he told his wife after browsing through the gallery.

"She really is marvelous," a tall, large-boned woman in a white tuxedo was saying. "You must be very proud."

Nathan turned to reply. "Yes, of course," was all he could manage. The sentence he wanted to say was much too complicated. How to reply to Nina Phillips's compliment of the bizarre sculptures which, he thought, revealed his wife's yearning for the very organ Nina had . . . the organ *Philip* had. . . ? Oh, the hell with it, Nathan decided.

Nina had settled in New York. She'd purchased a thriving midtown ophthalmology practice, determined to enjoy the serenity she'd struggled so hard to achieve. Children loved her light, humorous approach and so pediatric ophthalmology had become her subspecialty.

But serenity still eluded her. She dated men: athletes, doctors, entrepreneurs. She told them everything right away; no deceits, no heartaches, she reasoned. Many genuinely liked her, she knew, but Nina was a profoundly intelligent and perceptive woman and it soon became clear that she would never feel loved by any of these men. She would always be a curiosity, a badge they could award themselves. Even the most earnest, those who appreciated the subtle rewards of undressing her, making love to her, even they were subject to self-congratulation. And for Nina, that ruined everything.

There was, of course, her work.There was also tennis, playing and coaching, some small measure of celebrity. There was friendship, scattered and usually unfulfilling. And there was that one friendship that had endured from its unpromising beginnings: There was Carla.

Some evenings, they met for dinner and a movie. Sometimes they attended a lecture. On other evenings they dined at Nina's apartment. A salad, wine, conversation. Nina stretched her long legs out onto the glass coffee table; Carla sat opposite in a deep, comfortable chair. It might have been Homecoming weekend at Yale, she might have been planning to wear the powder blue suit tomorrow. Nina still loved her in that shade. Often, she wore the bracelet with the Yale key.

"Tulips!" Nina exclaimed when Carla thrust the bouquet at her. "You know how much I love these. Red tulips in a slightly overheated apartment go mad in no time, twisting and bending, just begging for van Gogh to capture their torment. Oh God, Carla, I love red tulips! You know I do!" She set them in a wide glass vase to give them room to "go mad."

"Alex is back from Italy again," Carla said when the two of them were in the kitchen fixing dinner. "She's had every grant imaginable for that dissertation of hers and it's still not done. When will the foundations wise up to all those Art History majors hanging out in Florence, sipping *caffe latte*?"

"I'm glad she's back," Nina said. "You've missed her."

"You're sweet," Carla said, "but you know, she's never really home anymore. She spends her time with Martin, that musician who's hung around her since high school, and with Nathan. He's become part of their circle now. Heaven only knows how he managed that."

"He loves music."

"He loves their youth, their language. He even loves their dungarees. It's understandable enough: He loves their energy. I just don't know what *they* see in *him*."

"He's erudite. He tells a good story and," Nina nudged a wide elbow into Carla, "he pays for their dinner. Do you suppose you're jealous?"

"Frankly, yes, a little."

"But you *do* have Lisle," Nina reminded her.

"Lisle saved my life," Carla said. "She really forced me to be an artist."

"She's a great kid, Lisle, and Alex may yet return." A long arm wrapped itself around Carla's shoulder and drew her to the large rib cage with its small soft breast.

"You're the best of everything now," Carla told her friend. "A loving mother and still. . . ."

"A protective man?"

"Well, something like that. What I mean is you're still the same. It's hard to say this after all you've been through, but to me you're still the same old Phil."

Nina released her and turned to opening the wine. They carried a yellow salad bowl, two matching plates, and the wine to the living room, and set up dinner around the tulips.

Silence. It was common enough between them but this time it worried Carla. "Phil always loved red tulips," she said hopefully. "He loved red tulips and lots of scallions in the salad. Do you want me to ignore all that?"

"I'm not denying what you said," Nina said. Her gaze rose above Carla's head and lost itself in the bright dots of light beyond the window. Then she tucked her chin down abruptly and focussed, once again, on Carla.

"How's Nathan doing?"

"You mean his health? He's coming along."

"I mean everything. Nathan. How's it going?"

"The same." Carla could not look up. "Worse," she finally whispered. "Much worse. His medicine has some awful side effects. It's really horrible now."

"You could still leave," Nina said. "Every day is the first day of. . .well, you know."

Carla shook her head. "It's gone on too long. I can't divorce him. I've made. . .how many stabs at it? And the girls. I couldn't do that to them."

"Perhaps they're angry at you for putting up with it."

"Do you think that's it? Really, Philip, I don't know how it got so awful. I never loved him. I've made such a mess!"

Nina pulled her knees up to her chin and then pushed them forward to stand up. She walked around the table and sat down beside Carla. "It's *all* a mess, this man-woman thing. Believe me, I know better than anyone."

Carla cocked her head and blinked hard. "Oh Philip, Philip! Why couldn't you have liked women? You're still my best friend, my best love. What an awful bungle!"

Nina reached out and pulled Carla's face toward her. She held it, stroking the shiny hair.

"You know," she began softly, "you're absolutely right about me. I *am* the same. I *am* still Philip. But you're wrong about me not liking women. I've always liked women, Carla. I've always *been* a woman!"

189

She sat back now and drew her knees up to her chin. "Philip wasn't gay, you know. He just had to spare you all this." She gestured vaguely around the living room. "I mean *this*," she said, finally pointing to herself.

"Anyway, the nasty thing of it is . . ." She pulled the salad plates together and stacked them in the empty bowl. She drained the wine from her glass and then from Carla's and then rose and carried the dishes to the kitchen.

Carla slid her feet back into the loafers she'd dropped under the table. "What?" she asked. "What's the nasty thing?"

Nina leaned across the counter that divided the kitchen from the living room and waited until she could fix Carla's eyes with her own. "The thing is, I am still Philip and I still love you." She paused to gauge the effect of her words.

Carla was looking up at her, tears welling in her eyes.

"It's not working out with men and me," Nina continued, softly, deliberately. "Over and over again I have to face up to the fact that sex with men is just no good."

"Poor Philip! After all you've been through!"

"Well, twelve years with the shrink and it's come to this, Carla. I *am* gay. I'm a gay woman. There, it's out."

Carla looked into Nina's face as long as she could bear to and then down at the floor. Finally, she turned her back and walked to the farthest corner of the room. She stood there, hugging herself tightly.

"Why is this harder for me than the sex change was?" she asked.

Nina shrugged lightly. "Perhaps my sex change made sense of things that puzzled you. It explained why we couldn't be together."

"And this?" Carla's voice was barely audible.

Nina was standing behind her now, her hands on Carla's shoulders. "This explains why we *can* be together. If you want to, that is."

"Philip!" Carla turned to face her friend. "I mean Nina. NINA!" She groped about for her purse, her coat, her gloves. "I'm sorry, I'm really very sorry. I have to go." She tucked her gloves into her purse and then pulled them out again. "Nathan will worry. I'm sorry, Philip. I really must go."

"Please don't be upset," Nina said. She stood, blocking Carla's path to the door. "I do love you, Carla. I always have, you know."

Carla began by reaching around the tall figure, groping for the doorknob. But in the end, her fists were on Nina; they pushed hard against her chest, they pummelled her.

Nina planted herself to receive the blows. "Please, Carla. I know this will take time. Just promise you'll think about it."

"Oh God!" Carla cried. It was a sound that welled up from the soles of her feet, her knees, that swirled furiously in her stomach, filled her chest to bursting and finally flew into the air. "Oh, God, Philip! ALL. . .THESE. . .YEARS!"

Thirty-five.

Even as the line she stood in inched its way toward the exit, Carla felt the Sarasota air condensing on her face, vanquishing the stale atmosphere of the Delta airplane with a tropical brew of coconut, orchid, and brine. She emerged into the smallish terminal, her linen suit lewdly wrinkled, her bone-colored pumps too confining, her hair rising up to meet the moisture with a fine halo of frizz. She'd visited Florida many times since Felix's death and still it was impossible to leave New York sufficiently persuaded of just how excessive her attire would seem on arrival. She smoothed her skirt under her as she entered the cab. High hedges of hibiscus, lurid palms, the thickly sweet, verdant smell of Florida in her nostrils. Perspiration on her brow and seeping through her panty hose.

The marble lobby at 1534 Gulf Drive was frigid and dry, and the acrid odor of chlorine wafted in from the pool at the rear. In what she had always thought of as an icy vault, this chemical smell seemed, to Carla, particularly horrid. She watched the lights move down the numerals over each of the two elevators, forcing her gaze away from the easel that stood in the center of the lobby. A chalkboard announcing the death yesterday of Leonard Marcus: Funeral services tomorrow. Edna and the family sitting *shiva* in apartment 5-E. A memorial service in the lobby next Sunday.

She stepped out of her shoes almost as Sophie opened the door to her, and gave herself over to her mother's hug, her questions about the trip, about New York. And yes, she had remembered to bring a can of those Italian biscuits Sophie so adored. And yes, she would love a shower. Immediately.

Throughout dinner, she was filled with unease. She was looking for an opening, the right moment to broach the only subject on her mind. Except for answering her mother's questions, she found she had nothing else to say. They finished their meal in silence and stood in an ancient arrangement, one washing, the other drying, the few dishes they had used.

Finally they were settled on the terrace, facing out to the Gulf of Mexico and the sultry city lights along the coast.

"Something is wrong," her mother said. It was not a question. "Tell me, *liebchen*."

"I've decided to leave Nathan," Carla said. She did not turn from the view beyond the terrace.

"That's impossible," Sophie declared.

"Nevertheless," Carla said flatly, "I'm getting a divorce."

"Whatever is troubling you, sweetheart, I know we can fix it," her mother said.

"I never loved him, Mother. I told you that before I married him."

"But since then. . ." Sophie began.

"It's gotten worse. You won't talk me out of this, Mother. I've come to tell you, not to ask permission. I know it hurts you. I hate hurting you. But it's a very good thing for me." Carla remained facing the Gulf, unable to turn to her mother.

"Your father loved that man like a son," Sophie murmured.

"I'm not so sure," Carla said. "One day, before he died, he apologized to me, you know."

"He didn't force you, *liebchen*. He loved you. And that other man from Yale. . .well, he wanted to save you from *that*."

Carla rose and began to pace the narrow terrace.

"This will be terrible for the girls," Sophie continued. "Alex so close to him and all."

"Alex is a grown woman, Mother. She can manage. Anyway, I'm convinced this is the best thing I can do for my girls."

Sophie rose now and stood in her daughter's path. "So! So this is what it's about!" Her voice was angry. "It's those feminist friends of yours! Those women running around by themselves. . ."

"This is a different world, Mother! I don't expect you to understand." Carla began to tremble as she realized she was shouting.

She left the terrace and pulled the leatherette room divider closed. In the space that was now her bedroom, she shed her robe and sank onto the lumpy mattress of the sofabed. She wrapped her arms about herself and stroked her bare shoulders, her arms. She heard her mother pad to the bedroom and close the door. She was certain she was doing the right thing and yet, the pain in her mother's face . . . that gnawed at her. She lay flat and naked on the cool sheet, letting the air conditioner dry her skin. She thought how much she loved sleeping nude.

Toward dawn, she slipped back into her robe and walked out onto the terrace. The night air slicked a briny coat over her cool face. Soon, the sun coming up behind the building made the Gulf a wide plate of pink and orange and she could hear Sophie in the kitchen fixing breakfast.

"You know," Sophie said when she had finished her coffee, "these independent women who are your friends now are not such a happy lot. What will you do, a woman alone? How will you keep those wonderful friends you and Nathan have? They won't be so nice when you're not married anymore."

"I don't want the Peekskill people, Mother. I don't want to live out my days catering parties."

Sophie poured them each more coffee. Her hair had been pinned hastily into a bun atop her head and wiry white strands stretched out crazily all around it. "Have you thought about money?" Her tone was grave. "You've had a comfortable life, my darling. The best clothes, the best schools. The house in Peekskill is yours, of course, but the apartment. . ."

Carla set her cup down noisily. "You've had a terrible night, I can see. I'm sorry to upset you so, but I'm going to be fine, Mother." She took her coffee to the terrace and slid the screen shut behind her.

When Sophie reemerged, she was bathed and dressed in a cool green cotton shift. Her still-wet hair was meticulously rolled into a twist and carefully pinned. The toenails protruding from her white summer shoes, Carla noticed, had been painted with mauve enamel. She had never seen her mother with painted toenails.

Sophie beckoned her daughter to the far end of the terrace. "See down there, around the pool," she said. "Women, only women. They swim a little, they play cards. The men—what's left of them—hardly ever come out. You think this is a nice life?" Carla remained silent. "This is *not* a nice life," her mother continued, "living out your years alone, playing cards with the ladies! Not nice at all."

"Mother, if you'd like to come back to New York, to live with me. . ." Carla began.

"Not me!" Sophie fairly shrieked. "I'm an old woman. But *you*. You think fifty-year-old men grow on trees? You think they're so wonderful, the ones that are left? You're a beautiful woman, you'll have no trouble. But you think they're any better than what you have?"

"I don't need a man, Mother."

"Those new friends of yours have made you very foolish." Sophie shook her head. All sadness and dismay.

Carla leaned toward her, intent on keeping a soothing voice. "I have my work, Mother. I love my work. And I make money from it. My sculpture is selling very well now. You should be proud."

Sophie's shoulders hung low, her chin rested on her chest. She was struggling to accept the new shape her world had suddenly assumed.

"Do you think it's easy to live without someone to love you? Since your father died, it's terrible. I read, I keep everything neat. I have new friends down here, all very nice, very cultured. Many Europeans. But I miss your father!" Heavy tears rolled over the creases of her face.

"I know," Carla said softly, "I miss him too."

"You need someone, *liebchen*. Besides your work, you need someone to love you. Someone to have coffee with in the morning, someone to sleep with you at night, to make you comfortable. You have so many years ahead of you. You think that Szabo man. . ." Sophie stopped abruptly and turned away.

"Tom?" Carla said. "What about Tom?"

"Nothing. Just your father thought. . ."

"I said good-bye to Tom years ago, Mother."

"So it was true, then."

"It's over."

"Then you do need someone."

Carla remained quiet, staring out across the Gulf. Then she took her mother's hand in both of hers. "I promise I'll have someone to love me," she said.

So it was done, then, she thought as she settled back in the plane seat. She had explained that it would all take time. She would see a lawyer. She would speak with her daughters. She would only tell Nathan when it was all in place. Tell him sweetly, firmly. He could call her if he became ill again. But she wanted everything settled before she told him.

195

"Poor Nathan," her mother had said.

This trip to Florida, Carla thought as she watched the orange streaks outside the plane's window turn to deep purple, this trip was the most difficult thing she'd ever undertaken. Causing her mother such pain! But apart from that portion of her that belonged to her mother, Carla felt light as a cloud. As the plane banked over New York Bay and the skyline of lower New York came blazing into view, she decided this was _not_ the most difficult thing. The most difficult part of her life, she was certain, was the part that was about to end.

Thirty-six.

Leon Sinrich's damp red face had become unbearable. Perhaps it was the contrast with the celadon green of the new enamel cabinets. Nathan suggested lunch at The Oyster Bar.

"I've done the numbers," Sinrich said. He was trickling yellow beer into a tall pilsener glass. "Surgery is your money tree, no doubt about it. If you don't do surgery, you can't make a living. The office practice is just barely breaking even. You remember, of course, I told you you'd have to make some changes."

"Sharing the office didn't work out," Nathan said. "I can't work with a partner. I'm not cut out for business arrangements."

"Why do you want to give up surgery anyway?"

"It's giving _me_ up," Nathan said. "I get the laser positioned and I realize I'm working on the one seeing eye this patient has. One false move and I blind him. Then I get chest pains. And that increases the chances I'll mess up."

"Too much exposure here," Sinrich declared. "You'll have to shut down the whole practice." He said it like a man deciding to move money from one bank into another. He had, after all, done the numbers.

"I could sell the practice," Nathan said.

"That's true," Sinrich agreed. His pinky jutted out as he held the glass to his lips.

"How much?" Nathan asked.

"Whatever the market offers."

They were, Nathan understood, playing at dominoes. Your turn, my turn. It came to nothing. It was a conversation in which words were merely little blocks of wood.

A speck, a tiny flicker at the periphery as he drove up the Szabos' driveway. An image that so countermanded logic, all his cognitive powers rose up to persuade him he had not seen it.

Nathan had been certain he would never see Vera again. He had fixed her as an idea, the conjunction of certain images. It had its own texture, its particular comfort, its particular bitterness. He conjured it at times as refuge and, at times, as self-flagellation. She had become an idea he could summon at will.

But it was actually Vera, now, sweatshirt and sweatpants, tearing across the Szabos' backcourt on this chill March Sunday. Running to return Armand's backhand. Nathan could make out the broad smile as her racquet smartly addressed the ball. It was Vera. The long, dark braid gone, her hair cropped close, tinged with grey. Still the wiry little body, charged with energy. He could see this through the naked vines that clung to the Szabos' fence, awaiting spring.

"Is that Vera?" Carla asked. "Armand never mentioned it."

Carla opened her arms to Vera and planted a kiss on her cheek. "Welcome back!"

She's a real thoroughbred, my wife, Nathan thought. "Good to see you again," he managed to say.

After lunch, Nathan suggested they play doubles. "I'm out today," he told Tom, "but you and Tilly can play Carla and Armand."

Vera settled herself in the chaise longue beside him. Still mischief in her face. And the huge grey eyes, still sparkly.

"How have you been?"

"Just fine," he said. "Better than ever, in fact. Your tennis strokes looked pretty good."

"I had a good teacher." She winked at him. And then her brow furrowed as he had seen it do so many times. "But you're not playing," she said. "Are you well?"

"Yes, yes. I told you. Better than ever."

He had never had to consider it, yet it was instantly clear. So much had happened since last they spoke. Things she would not ever need to know. He would never tell her all those things. Knowing them now, what did it matter? He could tell her what he wanted her to know. Which was very little, and that would do. They would speak of her. *She* would be their subject that afternoon.

"My research ended," she said when he asked. "The grant just ran out."

"Ah, Vera. I know how you feel," he said. He pulled the zipper on his parka up close to his chin.

"Actually, I think you'd be quite surprised," she said. "I'm still at Columbia, but I'm a student now. I'm studying to be a rabbi, Nathan."

Was it her density, her mass that suddenly altered? Nathan knew it was something fundamental. Her shape? And the light falling across her, was that also transformed? Perhaps he had been right to believe he would never see Vera again. He fastened on the steady pinging of the ball on the court beside them.

"You must be the only woman at the seminary," he heard himself say.

"Not at all," she laughed. "They're entrusting quite a few of us with the eternal flame these days."

"I'm not sure they should do that," he said. "Eternal matters are better entrusted to men."

Vera turned that ironic smile on him. "Are men more trustworthy?"

"We're dealing with immortality here," he said. He was remembering Colby on the ski lift. "Men, you know, are frantic on that subject."

She was still smiling. "I'm sure that explains their perpetual insecurity and considerable aggression, but I doubt it contributes much to their holiness."

"Nevertheless, we do worry about it," he said, "and now women are being ordained when they don't really understand."

"I'm just hoping to preserve what's preservable," she said.

"Which is what?"

She thought for a moment. "A sense of spirituality," she said. "I think I can be entrusted with that."

"You'll do well at that, but it's not what I want to have preserved."

"I know."

Tom and Armand were engaged in a disagreement about a serve. Their voices were audible but not their words. In the time he had purchased to become accustomed to her again, it became clear to Nathan that Vera was still vibrant and supple as ever. More supple than he had imagined, in fact. And there was something powerful in her now, something that had not been there before.

He decided to tell her about the Bergs.

"A couple in the office building offered to buy me out," he said. "A hundred thousand dollars. Can you imagine? My whole life for a hundred thousand. I'd rather send it all up in smoke. Forty years building a practice for a lousy hundred thousand?" He paused, out of breath. "So I told them to go fuck themselves," he said.

"Nathan, you didn't design cathedrals or compose music. You didn't choose to build something durable. You healed and comforted hundreds of people."

"And then they died anyway," he said. "I should have been an architect. Should have put my efforts into something that would last." He pulled his hood up over his head.

The sun had begun to sink and the temperature was taking a sharp turn. Vera suggested waiting inside for the others to finish their game.

"You keep wanting to stop the river from flowing," she said when they were settled in the Szabos' study.

199

"That's understandable, isn't it?"

"If you had become an architect, do you think that would have stopped the river? Years from now, people would pass your building. They'd think to themselves, that's a great building. Then they'd think about something else. Or they'd think about your name and *then* they'd think about something else. The building, your name, would be floating past them in the stream of experience." Her long fingers rippled through the air. "Floating, flowing. There's no way to stop the river, Nathan."

"This isn't very comforting news." He had set two brandy glasses and a bottle of Remy Martin on the little table between them and poured them each a brandy.

She reached across and took his hand. "I'm sorry, Nathan. It *is* very hard. Of course you shouldn't sell your practice for a lousy hundred thousand."

"What *should* I do, rabbi?" he asked.

Vera thought for a bit and then hunched her shoulders up in that familiar shrug and laughed. "Give it away," she said, "and then move on."

"Too late," he said. "Nowhere to move."

He poured himself a second brandy and told her of his nights among Derrida, Wittgenstein, and Duras. He really was feeling fine, he said. The surgery had been a huge success, and his tennis game, he assured her, was strong as ever. "Except that sometimes I lose to Carla."

"How is Carla?" she said. "I mean Carla and you. . ."

"I have no life with Carla," he said flatly. "It's one thing that has never been right."

"You've never wanted to change it, though. All these years, and with all your options. Something's kept you there."

He looked down at the snifter in his lap. "I had to stay," he said. "I'm a coward. I had no choice." He thought he might tell her of his trip to Gerald's office, of the color of Gerald's face. But telling her now, what was the point? It was one of those things she did not need to know.

She sat back in her chair and studied him thoughtfully.

That same intent gaze he'd seen at the Matisse exhibit, pondering anemones. Then, as though she'd reached a decision, she leaned toward him.

"Nathan," she said. "I've thought about this quite a lot and I've never understood it. All you ever seem to feel for Carla is contempt. I think you've spent your entire life with someone who has only your contempt."

Nathan rested his face in his hand. His cheek was damp, his eyes hot. "It's true," he said at last. "Contempt is exactly what it is."

"I don't understand it," Vera said.

Nathan pulled a handkerchief from his pocket and mopped his face, studied the glass in his hand. "It's easy, Vera. Contempt, I mean. It's just so easy." A long swallow of brandy. "I don't try to figure her out. I don't worry about what she wants from me. So long as I show up when I'm expected, I can pretty much ignore the rest. The singular virtue of contempt, I suppose, is that it's so very easy."

He threw his head back, drained the snifter and looked at her. "Funny," he said. "I never thought about it that way before."

He had been astonished, once, that Vera's eyes could be clear as crystal and soft as velvet all at once. Her husky voice was wistful now, hesitant. "You don't engage yourself. Not deeply. Is that what you mean?"

"It's lonely, of course," he said, "but perfectly undemanding. A coward's bargain." He looked up, determined to look at her as he spoke. "*You. . .*could never be so easy," he told her. "*You. . .require* a response. Engagement, as you put it. And so for me, Vera, you will always be. . ."

"What?"

"Impossible."

Vera said nothing. Nathan fumbled with the bottle and poured a snifterful.

"That's a lot of brandy," she said.

"You know," Nathan resumed, gesturing broadly with his glass, spilling liquor on the Szabos' kilim rug, "I've spent most of my life avoiding real emotion."

Vera frowned and remained silent.

"Well, I'm not without feelings, of course, he continued. "Envy, ambition. Man-stuff, you know. Strive, compete, achieve." His vowels were long, his consonants slurred.

"I've been an idiot," he said. "Been wanting the wrong thing the whole time. The wrong thing. What I really should have been wanting. . .what I really want. . ." He paused, his glass wavering in midair.

He rearranged himself, straightened in his chair. "I want to be like you," he blurted. "Spontaneous, like Vera. Alive, like Vera." His voice dropped. "Never really felt alive, you know."

He rose to his feet and began pacing. "Goddammit, Vera," he sputtered, "helluva thing to know this now!"

He paused in front of her, his voice almost a whisper. "That river of yours, Vera. It flows by mighty quickly."

He noticed her glance across to the doorway. Armand and Carla and the Szabos tumbling noisily into the room, chilled, perspiring. Tilly would set out some of those smeared-over canapés. Nathan tossed the remaining brandy down his throat and blinked.

Thirty-seven.

Along the Henry Hudson Parkway, yellow-green knobs rose on the cherry branches, but charred lodes of ice flanked the roadway. Winter was no longer bearable. Spring had yet to appear. Nathan had seen this season too often before. He was heading into New England, his skis bound to the roof of his car.

The Holyoke Range was freshly white. He stopped in Northampton for gas. Luce's chalet restaurant had long ago disappeared. He slammed the car door hard against the cold. The "Kyrie" of Mozart's *Requiem* was on his tape deck. For the angels. He drove north into Vermont.

White as bedlinen. As thirsty towels. Whiteness glistening. Bath foam on his wife's shoulder in Truro. White foam
slithering over Vera's ankle in a room that smelled of fruit.
Ahh, they had said. Ahh! The white, the glistening.
Enduring snow. Stoical as the sea.
Boys on snowboards whooshing past. Truculent,
immortal boys. Could they imagine peril? He would have
done just that at their age. When I am again that age, he
thought. Impossible.
But days such as this: days of light. Unceasing reverberations of whiteness, maddening almost as church bells in
a tiny town pealing all at once. The cloying sunlight of July.
The delirium of whitenesses of days such as this.

The squeak of ratchets as the little chairlift came round
the bend. Then it tucked under his thighs and scooped him
up over the hemlocks. Colby hadn't needed to be chief. His
research had been enough. Colby wrapped in gauze, flaking
away under snow white gauze. I should have been chief,
Nathan thought. Impossible, now. Even with Heaney retir-
ing. They'll take a younger man. Someone who advertises.
A speech for Heaney on his retirement. Not quite a eulogy.
A fountain pen when he'd finished his internship. Crackling
new spine on the blue *Directory of Physicians and
Surgeons*. And Felix: *Katte*, who may have survived.
The pulley halted and the slatted bench swayed over a
gorge. She had seemed a child, covering her eyes, the warm
pressure of her face buried in his shoulder. Supple woman,
gypsy woman. Velvet eyes, velvet dress. And peonies they
were, carmine and rose. Heady June peonies splayed among
feather beds. An odalisque. It was not possible to be her.
Not possible to have wanted that.
He slid off the lift chair and crouched slightly, gathering
momentum for the turn to the ledge. An eggshell surface
and powder just beneath. A good day to have closed the
office. The mountain belonged to him. And to the truants on
their snowboards. He grasped his poles and pushed off. A
hole in his right mitten, his index finger growing numb. The

trail slick where intermittent sunlight pressed it into water and then abandoned it to the wind. Harsh wind. It made his eyes tear at the plateau and he paused to adjust his goggles. Her eyes were watery with cold and her cheeks were crimson with it as she pressed forward, her hands buried in a fur muff. A fur muff that suited her so perfectly. . . .

A narrow trail off to the left. He could not recall the map. He'd see where it led. A long flat ribbon of fresh snow through the hemlocks. An ancient forest. Thick fragrant wood. Lew Perrin and Tilly Szabo slumped in redwood chairs beside the new tennis court, sipping iced tea. Sweet, ebullient Marian, how Lew delighted in her. Iced tea among the pear trees hung so low with fruit.

Before him, no trail. The back of the mountain, a bowl of sorts, undulating into the horizon. He would make painstaking, delicate work of it. In perfect form. Form counted for so much more than Tom could ever imagine. Fine dancerly labor, carving perfect esses down the mountain. Turning precisely where he chose to turn. Light pressure on the downhill ski. A tiny graze of the pole's tip, exquisite rotations. His father could never understand.

Careful, studious work. The rhythmic, repetitive work of an orchardier. Muriel at her piano. Slim fingers of astonishing strength. She stood to play Lizst. The hourliness, the dailiness, the monthly, yearly, endlessness. The attentiveness opening into rapture. She had been possible. The impossibility had been in him.

An exhilarating run. He released his skis. A twinge in his chest as he bent to lift them to his shoulder. He'd need to hike around the base to find the chairlift again. That bowl, so surprising, so rewarding. He sat on a pile of sawn logs. A small rest. He pulled his turtle over his mouth. Breathe some warm air. Quiet the twinges.

And now, the chairlift in view.

"Found the little trail to the back side, eh?" The lift engineer was happy for conversation.

"Gorgeous spot," Nathan said. "Not too many customers today, huh?"

"Slow, Wednesdays. End of the season. And cold, hey?"

"Beautiful, though. Worth putting up with the cold."

"Beautiful it is," the man agreed.

Nathan placed his skis on the ground and planted his boots in their bindings, snapping each lock forward.

"Better make this your last run," the engineer said. "Not enough action to keep this thing grinding anymore."

"Never say 'last,'" Nathan said.

"Okay, pal."

The sun was at mid-March four in the afternoon. Slanted columns of light sifting through the hemlocks. Sunbeams a child might grasp in his hand. Cylinders of windblown snow. Polka dots on organdy. And freckles on her back. He thought it was too much to know this. Once more at the ledge, he tucked his chin down to catch the warmth of this own body. Warm his throat, his chest. He pushed off.

The lining of his mitten had torn clear through. Cold fingers. Once he'd had no feeling at all in those fingers. Cut them to ribbons for want of feeling. Nitroglycerine in his zippered pocket. Just in case. Holding Alexandra's chubby wrists above the harpsichord keys so her stout little fingers just touched them. The C-major Prelude and Fugue. She deserved a fine boyfriend, this curly-headed daughter. You deserve to be happy, she'd said. *Tekiah! Teruah!* he'd sung out to her. And Vera's face behind the candle flames, long fingers beckoning the tallow smoke.

Promise me, Lisle, golden peach of a child, that you will never be older than seven! How extravagant, that wide winter sky! Bejewelled with Wittgenstein and Paul DeMan and Marguerite Duras. He was precluded. Such yearning! Enough to make a man's heart ache. An ache like the door of a bank vault, closing against his chest. At the little trail off to the left, he would stop for nitroglycerine. He had been shorn. Shorn of his chest hair, shorn of his pubic hair. Shorn of all his colored leaves.

His fists tightened on the poles. Sunlight on the wane. He'd forgo the pills. The bowl just ahead. An easy waltz down the spill of white glaze. Stripes of hard-edged sunbeams and partway down a little stand of trees, a small dark island in the slick white sea. He had not noticed it before.

The door to the vault slammed into his chest, knocking him down, his head and shoulders shattering the icy crust. His right ski snapped loose and slid silently away. The left binding jammed and held its ski now scraping loudly alongside him, holding his left leg up almost perpendicular to his path of descent. He could not, he realized, snap his legs closed. He could not move his left leg, nor his left arm. They flailed, enervated, insensate, beside him. No longer him.

The little island of trees, he was bearing down on it now. He might try to pass it on his right, grab hold the birch at the tip of the island. If he could shake the mitten off. . .Open his hand and. . .the brightness gone.

Grey. The nurse had said he looked grey. The sky, the mountain too. Grey. Not the grey of vanishing sunbeams, not the grey of dusk. The grey of impossibility. His own grey impossibility. It was almost impossible to see.

The limp left leg with its clinging ski opened him to a vee as he careened toward the island of trees, its staunch birch standing watch. Impossible to draw his leg in. Impossible to shake the mitten, to steer his course. Impossibilities entirely within him.

All those things he wanted to tell her about how he had been then and at all times other than then. Things he might have told her had they had more time.

He could be impaled on the straight, watchful birch. At the uphill tip of the dark little island. Legs chevroned, sailing right into it. He hoped his heart would give out before then. Ischemia could keep him from feeling his testicles crush against the tree. Or perhaps the pain and its trauma would undo his heart's wiring and set off violent ventricular fibrillations. He could not decide which order of things he preferred.

Better a testicle than an eye? Better an eye than a heart? Better a heart than a testicle? Where, he wondered, where does a man really live? A heart in a box of ice. I cannot imagine such a thing, they had said.

Carla would be fine. Doctor father. Doctor husband.

Second doctor husband. A thoroughbred. He no longer heard his left ski strafing the ice. Silence.

Multifoliate ranunculae, musky blossoms, carmine and rose. And even now, he wanted to. . .yes, it might be his testicles first.
Where were those fibrillations? Those oscillations run amok? A dying star is no longer itself.
But, even now he wanted to
If only he could
If he could only smell
If
only
he
could
smell
her

Cold spaghetti &
tuna fish!